John and Cassandra
Fair is Fair

John Passfield

Rock's Mills Press
Rock's Mills, Ontario • Oakville, Ontario
2024

Published by
Rock's Mills Press
www.rocksmillspress.com

Note: The passages on the Trojan War are from *Chapman's Homer* (1616), as found on the Gutenberg Project site; the passages on the Ukrainian War are based on news reports of Thursday, February 24, 2022.

Cover: Craig Passfield
Cover Illustration: by John Passfield
Author's Website: www.johnpassfield.ca

Chapter 1
John 1

Sitting in my car beside the river. Sipping a coffee and watching the birds. They find a current and just sit on the water and float on by. Sipping my coffee and proofreading a chapter. Almost ready to send my new novel away. *Shakespeare and Cleopatra*. I keep reading it over and over. Soon be time to pick a new topic and start the writing process over again.

That invisible cave that no light comforts.

All the agony of the world since time began. Humankind suffering from forces which it can neither understand nor can it control. Happiness, oh of course, but only brief moments squeezed in amid the precarious circumstances and disastrous events that are the rhythm of what it is to be human here on this earth.

A man

A writer polishing a chapter.
A boy who will fall into a fire.
The wisdom of knowing one's place in the world.

sat down

Do you know what an image is?
Do you know how an image works?
Do you know what an image does?

to write a book.

A series of seismic impacts.
The whole story takes place in the mind.
Emotion gradually, dramatically intensified.

Reading a chapter of *Shakespeare and Cleopatra* by the river. Starting to think of other things. Certain ideas keep coming back to me. They've stuck in the depths of the mind for years and years. Maybe a novel based on the *Iliad*. More than once I've come back to that topic, but nothing so far. Couldn't think of a novel-shape for Cassandra. Not enough there to make the complexity of a whole book. Made her a folk-tale in this one. A layer of imagery in the image-pattern that Cleopatra makes of her own life.

Imposed infinite sorrows on the Greeks.

A novel snatched out of the headlines on the nightly news – circa 2022 – and imaged in the mythical characters and scenes of ancient Greek tales.

Helen seems to have been a girl who was born of mixed parentage.

Polishing the rough draft of my new novel.
Wondering what novel-topic to explore next.

A young god
was quite curious.

A wealthy yield - there will be creatures - soon i will be born - an unbandaged grief - won't let me alone - out of your hands - no presence at all - can't be altered - sometimes undermine themselves - the sources and the ideas.

The arrow sped
through the night.

So what is it about Cassandra? Why is she at the core of my thoughts? She was a pest to all who knew her. Wouldn't let them just live their lives. Kept reminding them of things they did not want to know. Perhaps Apollo as a character – the arrogant, domineering male. Would he unbalance the premise of the novel? – would he insist on seeing the story as his own?

Infectious sickness sent to plague.

Action and immediacy – every chapter a seismic shock. A nightmare to which John is a witness – interacting with timeless forces, as embodied in two characters – a human and a god. Unable, of course – is John – to either influence or control.

He set out on
a personal odyssey:

The flowing magma
didn't know whether to bury
the ocean.

to go as far
above Mount Olympus
as he could go.

There is light
and there is blood
thought the Being.

Cassandra was a girl who was a mortal.

He reached a fence
with a sign on the gate
that said:

A perfectly innocent person is being broken.
In such a situation the mind is numb.
A tragic conception lying deep in the poet's mind.

How to introduce the conversations? How to get my characters on and off the stage? Well – maybe just start in the middle of the scenes. Let the lights come up as they're talking. Maybe start each chapter in the middle – in medias res.
To death by troops the soldiers went.
A feast of imagery, for sure. Every level of the mind churning out images of agony and of pain. And somewhere in the mix, a tiny note of something positive – a note that travels through the novel like blood through a vein.

Andromache was a girl who was a mortal.

Birds floating along as the current takes them.
Fish swimming along at a lower depth.

'Beyond this Gate
No Olympian God
Is Allowed to Go.'

Open the heads - trying to make sense - so heavily on my mind - so solve the problems - wisdom was all around them - fall by the wayside - can't be realistic - won't have any idea - sitting in a rocking chair - a special military operation.

It was a story
that told itself.

I'd love to write a Cassandra-novel. Just not sure how it would go. What would be, I wonder, the sources – besides the *Iliad*, of course. I don't remember her getting much ink in those thousands of words.

All things are done by strife.

It needs to simmer for a while, as I consider some of the elements of the Cassandra-Apollo story. Have to brush up on my knowledge of gods and things.

He was a person in actual life.

Two snakes

Gods sending sunshine and rain.
A conception near to music.
The appearance of a god in disguise.

were hissing

Do you feel images hatching in your mind?
Do you feel the images swimming into clusters?
Do you feel the images forming intricate patterns?

in a corner.

Cassandra means something to me that I feel the urge to explore. Having all these terrible things happening to her. Out of touch with fellow humans and with the gods. Nowhere to turn – unless inside. Forced, perhaps, to descend right down to the molten core.

Their limbs to dogs and vultures gave.

But then – when would I write this novel? I've got a lot, already, on my plate. Every novel-topic lobbies to be my next. I can't forget that I'm seventy-six years old, with a dozen ideas or more, all waiting their turn on the runway. I should have started this novel-writing project in kindergarten, instead of dipping my pen in the ink-well at fifty-four.

Chapter 2
Apollo 1

Look here, John, Apollo is saying. This is Chryses, my aged priest. On his knees on the stony beach and praying to me. Agamemnon has taken my daughter. I asked her release in Apollo's name. For the ransom I offered to him, I received abuse. Agamemnon is a human, but he sees himself as a god. Your honour, O mighty Apollo, has been besmirched by the dishonour shown to your priest. I pray that you will visit a plague on the Argive fleet.

If thou wilt be safe, begone.

Why do you keep coming back, John? Yes, the name is John – I know it is. I have a memory which never lets me down. I am the one the gods all ask when there is doubt. Well – I keep telling you I'm busy. Right now I'm deeply involved in the war – the war at Troy. I don't have time for your petty concerns about what it is to be a human and alive. You have your lot in life and that is that. Your life will be your life until you die. If you want to influence the gods, don't come whining here to me. Go back to your country and make a sacrifice. Pick the god whose sphere is the one of your concerns.

He wanted to write

Explaining the meaning of a scene.
An unreachable depth in the mind.
Looking for someone in a crowd.

about the forces

And what about your own life?
Do you think about it from time to time?
What conclusions have you come to – if any at all?

that govern our lives.

Inherited doom, inherited situation, inherited character.
The most purely tragic situation is the flaw in the universe.
A disharmony in the cosmic makeup of things.

The new King mistreated his brother. He had his brother imprisoned. He had his brother chained to a wall. He had him fed with stale crusts of bread and only given occasional sips of water to drink.
The fires of death went never out.
I do not want to talk about this topic, John – my relationships with mortal girls. I do not see myself as a braggart, John, but if I just state the facts, inevitably it would appear like bragging to you. So that is why I put you off when you appeared before. This is such a minor topic. It is of very little concern. Let me simply say that I am busy – extremely busy – extremely concerned – with the Trojan War, and I do not want to talk about this human girl – what was her name? – Cassandra, did you say? The Trojan War is my main preoccupation for the foreseeable time – more time than you would care to spare in your mortal world. This girl – this girl, Cassandra – is not a preoccupation, for me, at all. In fact, I'm surprised that you – a male – should demonstrate such misguided – distorted – concern.

Some say that Helen was the daughter of a swan and a god.

Asking Apollo about his relationship with Cassandra.
Apollo directing my attention to the war.

I am tied to a stake! There are books piled up at my feet! They are piled up as high as to my knees!

To solve the problems - stayed in the egg - not truly free - know the patterns - give it my full attention - find a current - scrape away the husk - can't be changed - nowhere to turn - her life had changed.

So fell in Hector; and at him Achilles; his mind's fare was fierce and mighty, his shield cast a sun-like radiance, helm nodded, and his four plumes shook, and, when he rais'd his lance, up Hesp'rus rose 'mongst th' evening stars. His bright and sparkling eyes look'd through the body of his foe, and sought through all that prise the next way to his thirsted life.
Of all ways, only one appear'd to him, and that was where th' unequal winding bone, that joins the shoulders and the neck, had place, and where there lay the speeding way to death; and there his quick eye could display the place it sought, e'en through those arms his friend Patroclus wore when Hector slew him. There he aim'd, and there his jav'lin tore stern passage quite through Hector's neck; yet miss'd it so his throat it gave him pow'r to change some words; but down to earth it got his fainting body.

He listened in vain
for a sound.

Now watch my arrows, John, Apollo is saying. Stand right there and you'll have a good look. No human can match the skill that I can display. First I start with the mules and the dogs. Then the men I cut down in droves. Each arrow contains the force of a terrible plague. The skin turns black and puss oozes from suppurating sores. Each hit by an arrow produces, you see, a plague-ravaged corpse – along the beach you'll soon see flaming funeral-pyres. It's my way of reminding the Achaeans of the difference between a human and a god.

See disclosed the secret of Apollo's wrath.

You know, you don't seem to realize the implications of this, John, but the first time you came to see me, and raised the question of that girl, I decided to end your visits once and for all. I put my sword right through your back as you turned around. And here you are still standing – as much a pest as you were before. You have flesh – as I can see – but you don't seem to have a heart inside that lumpy bag of blood and cartilage and bone. You went on talking as if my sword was a figment of my mind. No human could have survived it. I have concluded that you are a god – a god in disguise. To what end I cannot now conceive. I do not always get along with the other gods.

"Explosions could be heard today in Kyiv, Odessa and several other Ukranian cities as Russian President Vladimir Putin declared the start of a 'special military operation' against Ukraine, the scope of which isn't immediately clear."

The falling rain
didn't know whether
to cover the land.

Hands are throwing books at me! A mixture of people and of gods! The pile of books is reaching to my knees!

Something to send
from the sun
to those below.

Cassandra was a mortal who was favoured by a god.

"It has been reported that Briseis is now a slave in the camp of Agamemnon. She was taken prisoner in the destruction of Lyrnessus and declared a spoil of war. Initially, she was given, as a reward for valour, to Achilles, but became a bargaining chip in a dispute between the two great men of war."

They pray only for what is possible.
May the ewes in the fields be fertile.
May the land be rich in crops.

Then one day the Royal Archivist found an old, faded parchment. It was the Last Will and Testament of their late, lamented father, the deceased King.
Sickness and battle lay such a strong hand on us.
Listen – I don't understand very much of what you tell me, John. I don't know 'channels' or 'communications satellites' or 'watching the news'. All I know is that you are telling me what it is to be human. To live on this earth and experience the catastrophes and the joys. Well – why should you be an exception? – you and those people with whom you live? – in this 'Canadius' or 'Canadia' or whatever you call the country in which you dwell. Do you think your land has been blessed by all of the gods? The gods squabble – the gods disagree. One will send sunshine and one will send rain. Find a cave in which to hide when it thunders – come back outside when the sunshine reappears. You humans complain when you break a fingernail. That's the way it is, John: ours to grant pleasure – ours to inflict pain; yours to enjoy or to suffer – yours to give thanks or to complain.

Andromache was not noticed by the gods.

Apollo is trying to evade the topic.
Insisting that Cassandra be the topic of our exchange.

Every book that I have read! All the literature of the ages! Telling me that the world I live in is on fire!

Neither human nor a god - out of touch - in vain the men assay'd - no way of knowing - relentlessly-human desire - don't even mention me - the agony of the world - we've not yet discovered - born of their noblest strains - didn't want to know.

Then triumph'd divine Achilles: "Hector," said he, "thy heart suppos'd that in my friend's decease thy life was safe; my absent arm not car'd for. Fool! he left one at the fleet that better'd him, and he it is that reft thy strong knees thus; and now the dogs and fowls in foulest use shall tear thee up, thy corpse expos'd to all the Greeks' abuse."
Hector, fainting, said: "Let me implore, ev'n by thy knees and soul, and thy great parents, do not see a cruelty so foul inflicted on me. Brass and gold receive at any rate, and quit my person, that the peers and ladies of our state may tomb it, and to sacred fire turn thy profane decrees."

It was bound
to happen that way.

Oh look! – Look here, John!, cries Apollo. See what I've accomplished? They are preparing a massive feast! I have forced them to acknowledge my fundamental power! Only by recognizing me – reaffirming my place in the universe – by an offering of meat and barley and wine – praising – fearing – me as a primary force that affects their lives – and begging that I will relent – can they ever hope to be free of my devastating plague!
Thy strength will guard the truth in me.
I have asked you repeatedly, Apollo, to relieve the curse on the girl, Cassandra. I see no reason why you would not be moved to consent. She has suffered enough, most people would agree, for whatever you might have taken to be her offence.

He became a character in a story.

They disagreed

Images that bathe and soothe.
A reminder of a forgotten truth.
A story told around a fire.

as to the message

Do you see yourself as on a journey?
Or simply sitting in a rocking chair?
Does life fly by, overhead, above the clouds?

that they had heard.

The Last Will and Testament, signed in the late King's own hand, enjoined that it was the dead King's express wish that from year to year the two royal sons would each take a turn at being the King.
His eyes sparkle like kindling fire.
Do I know more than does Apollo? I can't remember my Greek folk-tales. Does he know the whole story as it's playing out in time? Does he know, as he speaks to me, that Troy must fall?

Chapter 3
Cassandra 1

Now look, John! – look at this!, Cassandra is saying. This is me – sleeping on my bed. See how uneasily I am lying? I am tossing and turning – not asleep, but not awake, as you can see. Now see what happens as I toss and turn. You can see faintly, by the light of the moon that shines through the window. Two snakes – one from either side – crawling across the surface of my bed – making their way, as I am writhing, towards my ears. See – I seem to be in a trance – I don't wake up the whole time. I don't stop writhing the whole time this is going on. And now those snakes are whispering – do you see? – see the flickering tongues? Those snakes are whispering their prediction in my ears.

Never good came from thee towards me.

So it's you again, John. I haven't seen you for a while. I wondered whether you had gone away. I have looked for you in the throne room – at the temple – in the crowd at the palace gates. You are the only one who will listen to what I am saying. I get tired of people who turn their backs and walk away.

But he knew nothing

A girl explaining a scene.
Anguish written on a face.
A huge rock rolling down a mountain.

about the subject –

Do you feel images swarming under the surface?
Do you feel images swimming in myriad schools?
Do you feel images sensing they're under attack?

nothing at all.

The theme of the profoundest tragedy.

What the tragic poet knows.
That the universe cannot be explained.

Oh why do you believe me? Why do you believe me when no one else does? Why are you, alone, exempt from Apollo's curse? My family is becoming quite hostile. They pray to the gods for future favours, but they don't want to know what is coming next. So far it's only been small things, but the predictions are getting darker – more ominously sinister day by day. The snakes are hissing that there's going to be a major prediction about Troy. You are the only one who believes me, John. Do you know how refreshing that is? Can you tell the people of the palace? – my parents and their advisors – make them believe me when I talk? Do you think that you could persuade them to listen to you?
Do not deceive yourself.
They have made amazing strides in the alteration of DNA.

Every writer had a story to tell of Helen. No two writers could agree on Helen's name. Some called her Helen of Sparta. Some called her Helen of Argos. Many writers chose to call her Helen of Troy.
Helen lying on a blanket in a cradle. Being cooed to by one of the palace girls. Milk dribbling from her cheek and from her chin. Trying to make sense of the gossip of the nursemaids. Something about the mating of a god and a swan.

Cassandra explaining to me about her visions.
How the snakes come and whisper in her ears.

Strum on the lyre
my ancient one
though it has
a broken string.

The accumulated misery - you should be grateful - the truth of the matter - the question is - will still be valid - besmirched by the dishonour - what it is to be human - lucky and unlucky - has the final say - in the noble cause.

This said, he left her there, and forth did to his bellows go, appos'd them to the fire again, commanding them to blow. Through twenty holes made to his hearth at once blew twenty pair, that fir'd his coals, sometimes with soft, sometimes with vehement, air, as he will'd, and his work requir'd. Amids the flame he cast tin, silver, precious gold, and brass; and in a stock he plac'd a mighty anvil; his right hand a weighty hammer held, his left his tongs.
And first he forg'd a strong and spacious shield adorn'd with twenty sev'ral hues; about whose verge he beat a ring, three-fold and radiant, and on the back he set a silver handle; five-fold were the equal lines he drew about the

whole circumference, in which his hand did shew (directed with a knowing mind) a rare variety.

He received
no confirmation.

Now come and look at this, John. Cassandra waves me over to stand by her side. Here you see the walls of Troy – and I am standing with my parents and others of note. See – the tall old man is my father, King Priam – the King of Troy. And the lady beside him – her favourite brooch is catching the sun – is my mother, Hecuba – the Trojan Queen. Andromache holds Hector's son on her hip. She always stands on the left as they face the crowd. I am telling them my prediction – what the snakes have told to me. You can tell by my face the anguish that this prophecy has caused. When I woke up it was as clear as if it was chiseled on tablets of stone. I tell them that Hector must never fight with Patroclus – never meet him man to man. I tell them as clearly as I can – in the simplest words. You see me turning and pointing – down at Hector – as I talk. A Hector-Patroclus encounter would ensure the destruction of Troy. I beg them to believe my every word.

'Tis not your swift foot can outrun me.

You know, John, I can see the past and the future of everyone here at Troy, but I can't see a thing where you are concerned. You are beyond my powers of discernment – a creature of another realm. You mentioned 'Canada' to me, once before, but I know nothing about that place. In fact, I heard nothing of what you said beyond that word. For a moment, when you first appeared, in the palace garden, I thought that you were a god in disguise. I asked you, remember, to speak to the other gods.

"Loud explosions could be heard in the direction of Kyiv's Boryspil airport shortly after Ukraine announced the closure of its airspace. Blasts are also being reported in the eastern Ukrainian cities of Kharkiv and Mariupol."

There will be creatures
wise and foolish
thought the magma.

I could ask Apollo to solve the problem of global warming.

Each to give
is a blessing –
a form of life.

Apollo looked in the mirror. He was first among the gods. He was handsome, intelligent, charming. He was considering a gift for his intended. He was head over heels in love with a mortal girl.

Cassandra would surely be attracted. Apollo was first among the gods. No mortal girl could resist him. He had always had his way. He felt he knew the way to win this girl.

"Sources have reported the cause of the prolongation of the war is that there is a division in the Achaean camp. It would seem that Agamemnon, the defacto leader of the Achaean forces, is at odds with the most effective warrior on that side, the great Achilles. It is not known what caused the breach, nor whether the two can reconcile their differences, but there is no doubt, our sources tell us, that the inability of the two Achaean leaders to coordinate their efforts has led, in the short run, to a seemingly-endless prolongation of the war."

The hero is isolated before some awful rift in the universe.
He looks into the chasm that must engulf him.
There is no issue which is free from potential disaster.

You appear and disappear. You are here and then you are gone. You seem to have no mortal existence. To me you seem like a god. I am sure, sometimes, that you are a god in disguise. I sense your empathy, your kindness, your concern. Please, John – use your influence in the conclaves. Speak to the other gods of the pain which accompanies Apollo's curse.

Myself will enter personally on thy prize.

They can alter one's DNA to make it so one can think like a creature at the bottom of the ocean – to think like a creature from outer-space.

Andromache is a character in the *Iliad*. Andromache is a character in the story of Troy.

Andromache holding the plumed helmet. Her husband hugging their little boy. She has the armour polished to a turn. She doesn't tell her husband. As she worked, she cut her finger on his sword.

Cassandra telling me of her anxieties.
Asking me to speak to the gods.

Strum on the lyre
which you have rescued
from the debris
as the city burns.

A tale of Apollo and his human.
A tale of Cassandra and her god.

The blood-soaked centuries - too much a failure - dramatically intensified - the wretchedness of my life - have come to believe - be a human and alive - trapped in a cul de sac - it's hard to be sure - to solve the problems - what i could mean.

For in it he presented Earth; in it the Sea and Sky; in it the never-wearied Sun, the Moon exactly round, and all those Stars with which the brows of ample heav'n are crown'd, Orion, all the Pleiades, and those sev'n Atlas got, the close-beam'd Hyades, the Bear, surnam'd the Chariot, that turns about heav'n's axle-tree, holds ope a constant eye upon Orion, and, of all the cressets in the sky, his golden forehead never bows to th' Ocean empery.

Two cities in the spacious shield he built, with goodly state of divers-languag'd men. The one did nuptials celebrate, observing at them solemn feasts, the brides from forth their bow'rs with torches usher'd through the streets, a world of paramours excited by them; youths and maids in lovely circles danc'd, to whom the merry pipe and harp their spritely sounds advanc'd, the matrons standing in their doors admiring.

Not a beginning –
not an ending –
not a turning-point in between.

This is the throne room, John, here at Troy, Cassandra is saying. There is my father on the throne. You remember my mother from the previous scene you observed. They are wondering what to do about my prediction. They cannot bring themselves to believe in the death of Troy. All their hopes are in Hector's prowess – he is their champion – their son. They are thinking that I am mad – I can read their minds, you see. They only tell me what they have agreed they want to say. My father tells me to listen, carefully, to what my mother is going to say. She is startled because he had said he would take the lead. Now he passes it off on her, as if a mother could soothe my agony. She fingers her broach as she sorts among the words. As if a mother could make Apollo's snakes go away.

Now put to sacred seas our black sail.

Apollo is the only one with whom I can interact. The humans, Cassandra – your parents – do not see me or hear me when I approach them. With the other gods, I have no presence at all.

He met other characters in the story.

Their assignment

A list of pertinent questions.
A girl gathering wild flowers.

A fatal decision to be made.

was to take a message

Are there images that are predators?
Are there images that are prey?
Is there a balance, do you think, in the image-world?

to a girl.

Perhaps I have cast myself in a story – a dream in which I'm a character in a book. But which of these two am I? A John-Apollo? – or a John-Cassandra? Just which character, in this story, will be the 'I'?
Thy service we must use.
But wait a minute – the advertisement cannot be right – we've not yet discovered a creature from outer-space.

Chapter 4
Apollo 2

Look John! – look! Patroclus is fighting like a lion! – Hector is wavering like a sheep!, cries Apollo. Hector doesn't see that Patroclus is not what he seems to be – Patroclus is wearing Achilles's armour and hefting his sword. Now watch me! – watch what I do!, shouts Apollo, and plunges in. He appears in armour and raises Hector's fighting arm. He points his sword towards Patroclus and Hector swells to the size of a god. Hector races into the thick of the din – his stallions snorting with scorching fire. Patroclus is ready for the combat – the two flail at each other with fury. Patroclus and Hector locked in the jaws of a deadly embrace. But then the deadlock is suddenly broken – Apollo attacks Patroclus from behind – knocks him off balance and Hector lunges. Patroclus is run right through the stomach by Hector's spear.

What a world of griefs this suit ask'd.

You know, John, I find you interesting – something new in my life. I have lived for thousands of years – for many millennia, as you claim to measure time. Yes, claim, John, as I don't believe you are human. I have decided that you are a god – a god in disguise. You are teasing me, in some unfathomable way. A rather irritating way, as I told you when last you were here. I am Apollo – I am a god – and I am not going to put up with being pestered – as seems to be your mission – to relieve such a minor curse on a mortal girl.

He had always sensed

A god interfering in a human altercation.
A failed image-pattern.
A girl writhing in a trance.

that there are forces

Who are the people that you have known?

What are the ways in which you have known them?
Are some relationships superficial and some for life?

acting upon us.

It is the essence of tragic thinking.
The solitary human faces his own destiny.
The inner-drama is playing out in his soul.

In outer-space the sugar cubes would float out of the bowl.
That thou might's see these holy acts performed.
Do you realize what I did for her? I gave her a power that no other human has ever had. I gave her the power to see into the future – to see seeds as mighty oaks – to see mountains as grains of sand and grains of sand as mighty mountains – to see rain when there is sunshine and to see sunshine when there is rain. The point that I wanted to make to her – the gift that I wanted to give – is the knowledge that no matter how bad things get – no matter the human griefs or trials – there will always be a future and you will be there. But now I hope the girl will suffer. I hope the future – which I don't control, of course – will be a cruel and miserable place for her to dwell. May her future be dark until the end of her days.

Helen gathering wild-flowers. Alone on a mountainside. Hugging a bouquet of colour to her bosom. I want to grow up and have a husband and many babies. Will I always be as happy as I am now?

Helen was the cause, some said, of the Trojan War. Others said that this was not the case at all. The Trojan War was due, some said, to many contributing factors. There was contention in the classrooms – there was debate beneath the trees. Was hers a story of contentious gods or of human flaw?

Apollo brushing my queries aside.
Insisting that I consider the events at Troy.

I am looking at a face! It seems to be more a mask than a face! The eyes are looking at me as if they would like to escape!

Follow the blazed trail - reconsider his role - a layer of imagery - have your lot in life - a stressful day - not asleep but not awake - not in evidence today - my essential self - cannot be sung - the nature of the world.

"Dog," Achilles replied, "urge not my ruth, by parents, soul, nor knees. I would to the gods that any rage would let me eat thee raw, slic'd into pieces, so beyond the right of any law I taste thy merits! And, believe, it flies the force of man to rescue thy head from the dogs. Give all the gold they can, if ten or twenty times so much as friends would rate thy price were tender'd here, with vows of more, to buy the cruelties I here have vow'd, and after that thy father with his gold would free thyself; all that should fail to let thy mother hold solemnities of death with thee, and do thee such a grace to mourn thy whole corpse on a bed; which piecemeal I'll deface with fowls and dogs."

Hector, dying, said: "I, knowing thee well, foresaw thy now tried tyranny, nor hop'd for any other law, of nature, or of nations; and that fear forc'd much more than death my flight, which never touch'd at Hector's foot before. A soul of iron informs thee. Mark, what vengeance th' equal fates will give me of thee for this rage, when in the Scæan gates Phœbus and Paris meet with thee."

All the arrow knows
is air, he thought.

I turned the tide of battle, John! I made Hector the better man! It was I who sent Patroclus to the grave! Now watch what Hector is doing. Come over closer, so you can see. What are the rules of honour in your city? – in your state? What in your state is the greatest insult that you can conceive? Hector is shouting at the Achaeans. He is defying them to attack. He says he will let the vultures have the body – let the vultures eat their fill. No burial – you see – no afterlife. Oh this has turned out just as I planned, John. There'll be no honour in death for Patroclus! Let the great Achaean warrior rot in the field!

Other here will aid and honour me.

Look – let's put this in a nutshell, John. A mortal girl – this girl, Cassandra – was lucky enough, as a human, to find that she was attractive to one of the gods. And not just any god – not a god of brute force or of trickery or one of those other unattractive forces, you understand – but the sun-god – the brightest, handsomest, most brilliant of all the gods – the son of Zeus and Leto, if you will. This put her in line to be the recipient of a cornucopia of supernatural benefits. And then what happened? – what did this silly, ungrateful, empty-headed girl go and do? Let's be blunt, John – let's be blunt. She shunned me – rejected me – gave me the heave-ho – turned me down. She weighed me in the balance, as if I were just another human. She didn't consider that she was dealing with one of the gods.

Feed thy heart with wrath.

But you know what's even more disappointing, John? – what thrust has pierced my armour? – what still bleeds as an unbandaged grief? To think that I chose her – I of the discerning judgment – of the eye that out-sees the hawk – the hawk that circles with deadly intent above the fields. That I chose a girl to admire who was completely unworthy – who I thought of as someone special – almost, it seemed to me, a female god – but who was merely a dim-eyed human – a limited, shallow, imperceptive human female after all. Who looked at me – the sun itself – while wearing a blind-fold – who chose to walk in the dung on earth instead of riding through the air on the arm of a god. Oh John,

I felt so foolish – she lit the fires of hatred in me. It was the gossip of the gods in the heavens – people on earth found out as well. To be humiliated by a slip of an earthling girl. There are issues of personal essence here – there is measurement at the core. To have seen light where there was darkness – to have seen sun where there was rain. So whose – John – was the greater failure of judgment – hers? – or mine?

" 'I have taken the decision to carry out a special military operation,' Russian President Putin said in a televised address, saying he was forced to act by claims of 'genocide' in Ukraine that have been refuted by neutral observers, including the United Nations."

There will be creatures
wise and foolish
thought the rain.

The face has a seam right down the middle of the nose! The seam opens up and the two sides of the face begin to peal away! There is a new face looking at me from underneath!

Each to deny
is a curse –
a form of death.

Apollo forced a gift upon her. He gave Cassandra a special power. It was the power to know the future. She had never asked a favour. She woke up one morning and knew that her life had changed.

Cassandra would toss and turn on her pillow. Lie awake until the dawn. Didn't want to know the future. Snakes would whisper in her ears. They would tell her every plight that would plague humankind.

"Apparently the spear entered the chest of Sarpedon and he fell from his chariot and expired in the dust. It is alleged that the spear that ended his life was thrown by the Achaean warrior, Patroclus.

The soldiers tell us that he gave instructions – did Sarpedon – as he was dying – as he was coughing up blood on the battlefield – that the brave Trojan warriors would fight on, in the noble cause – press on to victory, as it were, in his name."

The tragic movement is inexorable.
It is the only possible one.
It moves from foreboding to fulfilment along a straight line.

He found that if he held the sugar bowl upside-down the sugar cubes would not float out of the bowl.

Thou still art most my enemy.

I have always been very successful with mortal women. Their resistance invariably melts at the sight of me. Can you imagine what it feels like to have all the attributes of a god – and still be rejected? From the looks of you, John, I don't believe that you could possibly understand what I could mean. This girl – this slip of a thing – this merely human entity – this wretch – this Cassandra that you ask about – this little miss I-am-a-creature-above-the-gods – was the first mortal to take a pass on me. The relationship was a minor one, John, but a lesson must be taught. And – being a god, I have ways to make her pay.

The boy will remember this, she is thinking. He will remember all his days. His father in his armour as he waves. Hector in his chariot holding the reins. Andromache and Hector's son on the palace walls.

Andromache on the royal balcony. Standing beside the King and the Queen. Looking down at the crowd below. Standing where she always stands. Shaking her head as Cassandra relates her disturbing dream.

Apollo speaking of 'essences' and 'measurements'.
Sweeping Cassandra into a nutshell and casting her aside.

My own face feels quite odd! I feel it moving on my skull! My nose twitches as if there is a seam opening up from top to bottom! I fear that there will be nothing but a skull!

A feast prepar'd - and that was that - had to be told - sack of throbbing gristle - subject to a mixture - born of mixed parentage - swarming under the surface - one of your concerns - stereotypes and clichés - centr'd the circles.

Thus death's hand clos'd Hector's eyes, his soul flying his fair limbs to hell, mourning his destinies, to part so with his youth and strength. Thus dead, thus Thetis' son his prophecy answer'd: "Die thou now. When my short thread is spun, I'll bear it as the will of Jove." This said, his brazen spear he drew, and stuck by; then his arms, that all embruéd were, he spoil'd his shoulders of.

Then all the Greeks ran in to him, to see Hector's person, and admir'd his terror-stirring limb; yet none stood by that gave no wound to his so goodly form; when each to other said: "O Jove, he is not in the storm he came to fleet in with his fire, he handles now more soft."

Having been told
it had to happen.

Wait! – wait! Don't interrupt me, John!, Apollo is saying. There is something going on that I must see! Antilochus is racing across the beach. He finds

Achilles in the shadow of his ship. The same ship with the beaked prow which brought him to Troy. He is telling Achilles of the battle over Patroclus! Of the battle over the corpse that lies in the dust! Oh – I cannot believe this has happened! I did not anticipate – but now I see! The consequences will be terrible if I read this action truly! No doubt my participation in this battle will reverberate detrimentally on me!

What then lifts thy pride so high.

I can only repeat, Apollo, that I believe that you have done a grave injustice to the girl, Cassandra. Your greatness should be accompanied by magnanimity. You should release the girl as a gesture of universal accord.

The characters, presumably, had been people in actual life.

It was a message

An act that draws no profit after it.
A person who is tied to a stake.
Black earth turned up by the plough.

that had to do

Are there people who are mythical?
Who represent forces in your life?
Who embody your disappointments and your dreams?

with the fall of Troy.

But he kept forgetting to hold the sugar-bowl upright when his spaceship was landed safely back on the earth.
His heart bristled his bosom.
Oh I hope I'm not Apollo. He's the last character I would ever want to be. Surely the reader of a book should get to decide.

Chapter 5
Cassandra 2

The throne room at Troy. Sounds of fighting in the hallway. Flames are leaping from the curtains behind the throne. A giant timber comes loose and crashes to the floor. It catches Cassandra on the shoulder and knocks her down. She crawls across the marble and down the stairs. Shouting Achaeans enter the room. They smash the sacred icons and overturn the throne. She raises herself and staggers through the door. She stumbles through the ruins. Bodies of Trojans lie in the square. She hides in a doorway as the Achaean hordes rush by.

These thoughts strived in his blood and his mind.

I saw a shepherd, once, in the marketplace. Such are the visions that come to me, John. I broke from the royal train. I went over to him as he stood at the edge of the crowd. Your boy will fall in the fire, I said – you must never leave him alone. The shepherd was stunned. He didn't know what to say. A royal princess had deigned to speak to him. The others came over quickly. They hustled me away. Your highness neglects to be regal, they said – she must always take care to never forget herself.

Forces of benefit and ill,

A girl staggering through devastated ruins.
The question of who owns a story.
A queen tearing her royal garments.

forces of thunder and of rainbow,

Do you see images as friends?
Images that bathe and images that soothe?
Images that point to the paths on which you can safely go?

forces of sunshine and of rain.

It is a dramatic situation.
A strong character presses forward.
A fatal decision comes to be made.

They think that I am crazy, John – they think that I am insane. They are going to lock me up, of that I am sure. My parents don't wish to do so, but the advisors carry great weight. They claim to be in touch with the thoughts of the gods. My parents don't know what to say to me – they see me as lost to them. They have a war to fight and my problems simply complicate their lives. I fear that they will abandon me to the others. I fear that they will let me be put away. I have no idea of your powers. If you can speak to them, John, I pray that you will do so. Please John, make my parents understand.

Straight he knew her by her eyes.

He heard grunting as he turned the corner and walked in front of the bank. Two people were grappling on the sidewalk.

Helen at the head table of a banquet. Food and drink to tempt the palate of a god. How did I ever come to live in the land of Sparta? How did I ever get to marry Menelaus? It was never in my thoughts when I was a girl.

Helen looking with wonder at a golden apple. Each of the goddesses is splendid in her own way. I'm glad that I don't have to make that decision. I hear the prize is to be a beautiful woman. But why have I been asked to take part in this affair?

Watching Cassandra as the Achaeans ravage Troy.
Her passionate concern for a little boy.

What is the string
that is missing
from the lyre
that you rescued from the flames?

The mate of his soul - asked her release - your high-minded humans - the core of my thoughts - just state the facts - to live and to breathe - without a definite meaning - the profoundest tragedy - the sunlit performance - lesson must be taught.

Other where a solemn court of law was kept, where throngs of people were. The case in question was a fine, impos'd on one that slew the friend of him that follow'd it, and for the fine did sue; which th' other pleaded he had paid. The adverse part denied, and openly affirm'd he had no penny satisfied. Both put it to arbitrement.

The people cried 'twas best for both parts, and th' assistants too gave their dooms like the rest. The heralds made the people peace. The seniors then did bear the voiceful heralds' sceptres, sat within a sacred sphere, on polish'd stones, and gave by turns their sentence. In the court two talents' gold were cast, for him that judg'd in justest sort.

Perhaps, he thought,
the arrow is travelling still.

Cassandra is trapped in a cul de sac. An Achaean throws down his spear. He has found himself a royal Trojan spoil. He begins to unbuckle his armour. I won't be needing this shield. Make this easy – make this hard – either way is fine with me. Cassandra catches at a splinter – it is sharp with a jagged edge – a pole that was a prop for a vendor's shade. She holds it out in front of her – she thrusts it towards his eyes. He knocks her arm aside – he grins and thrusts her body against the wall.

I come from heaven to see thine anger settled.

There was a lady in the palace. Do you know what a waiting-lady is for? They help those of us who are regal to get through the day. Well I went over to her in the throne-room. All the business was done for the day. Both you and your daughter will come to survive this war. The lady was taken aback, John – she didn't know what to reply. In a moment I was surrounded and hustled away. Of course I didn't tell her – I didn't have the heart – that both the lady and her daughter were bound to be slaves.

"Hours after pro-Russian separatists issued a plea to Moscow for help to stop alleged Ukrainian aggression – claims that the United States dismissed as Russian propaganda – President Putin said he has ordered Russian forces to protect the people and demanded Ukrainian forces lay down their arms."

There will be creatures
lucky and unlucky
thought the magma.

I could ask Apollo to solve the problems of overpopulation and land, air and water pollution.

One of them
from the sun to the earth
must certainly go.

Cassandra spoke to Apollo. She tried to gently make her case. She would forgo whatever relationship he proposed. She didn't want to know the future – know the patterns of sun and cloud. Please ask the snakes to keep their thoughts to themselves.

Apollo was greatly troubled. Apollo was in a bind. He had given the gift of future-knowledge. He could not go back on his word. He was determined to not be bested by a mortal girl.

"We are told that Patroclus was run through with a spear by Hector. The Achaean warrior, dressed in the armour of the great Achilles, was distracted, it would appear, by the god, Apollo. The body of Patroclus, we are further told, will be left in the field as carrion for the fowl and the dogs."

A story of strong emotions.
A story of emotions about the events.
On the one side, rage and punishment – on the other, defiance and hope.

I wouldn't bother to talk to Apollo, John. He is arrogant, petty and cruel. Go directly, if you can, and talk to Zeus. Don't even mention me if you feel that it would undermine your suit. Ask Zeus to relieve the suffering – be sure to use the word 'please' – that the gods have visited on the people of the earth. Ask Zeus if he will – please – end this war. I would gladly sacrifice myself if my plight wrings any pity from the gods. Talk to Zeus – he is the chief god – he is the king of all the gods. He has the final say on everything they do. If you can persuade him, the other gods will fall into line.

If thy soul will use her sovereignty in fit reflection.

Beside the grappling culprits, on the sidewalk, were a gun and a sack of cash.

The fire burns hotter and hotter. The water hisses and steams and boils. My husband will be tired. He likes the bath to be almost scalding. The servants bring more wood from the outer room.

A messenger stands outside. He hesitates as Andromache works at the loom. He wipes his eye and shakes his head and grits his teeth. Andromache busily weaving the purple mantle. Yellow thread that makes a pretty border of flowers.

Cassandra trapped in a cul de sac by a brutal Achaean.
Soothing a mother who is worried about her child.

What is the note
that cannot be played?
What are the words
that cannot be sung?

A tale of Apollo and his human.
A tale of Cassandra and her god.

Mourning his destinies - wonder what it is - interacting with timeless forc-

es - the handle and the blade - this cycle of suffering - made of startled dust - tore stern passage quite through - what is coming next - only time can write - he has no idea.

The other city other wars employ'd as busily; two armies glittering in arms, of one confed'racy, besieg'd it; and a parlè had with those within the town. Two ways they stood resolv'd; to see the city overthrown, or that the citizens should heap in two parts all their wealth, and give them half. They neither lik'd, but arm'd themselves by stealth, left all their old men, wives and boys behind to man their walls, and stole out to their enemy's town. The Queen of martials, and Mars himself, conducted them; both which, being forg'd of gold, must needs have golden furniture, and men might so behold they were presented Deities. The people, Vulcan forg'd of meaner metal.

When they came, where that was to be urg'd for which they went, within a vale close to a flood, whose stream us'd to give all their cattle drink, they there enambush'd them, and sent two scouts out to descry, when th' enemy's herds and sheep were setting out. They straight came forth, with two that us'd to keep their passage always; both which pip'd, and went on merrily, nor dream'd of ambuscadoes there. The ambush then let fly, slew all their white-fleec'd sheep, and neat, and by them laid their guard.

Having happened
it had to be told.

So this is Old Priam's daughter, Agamemnon is saying. He is sitting on Priam's throne – scorched and battered amid the debris. You are the one they call Cassandra, so I am told. Well, you don't look like a princess. Are you sure you brought the right one here to me? I expected elegance – a bit of glamour – from a lady of the Trojan court. Not this waif in a sooty rag which she is clutching with those broken fingernails. Take your sleeve and wipe the grime from off her face. So what do you have to say for yourself, now, my cringing princess? Do you realize that the Achaeans are supreme? Well it can be death for you – or worse – if I so order. Your life is a bauble that I hold in the palm of my hand. I am the victor – my power is unlimited, my girl, where you are concerned. I could crush you as your Trojans sought to crush me.

All my powers inflame with contumelies.

I have solicited, on your behalf, the god, Apollo. I have asked him, repeatedly, to relent in this oppressive curse. Perhaps if I press your suit again, he will soften in his attitude towards your cause.

Actual life becomes a story when time has passed.

As sure as the sun, the moon and the stars,

Plenty of topics to pursue.
A body defaced by fowls and dogs.
An estimate of all the wrongs in the world.

Troy will fall,

Do you see images as enemies?
Lying in wait along the trail?
Images demanding your money or your life?

hissed one snake.

I feel an affinity with Cassandra, but what do I say to her? In my family, you never lie to make anyone feel better. You never say, 'It'll be all right' because you don't know. You always say, 'It might be good and it might be bad.' But here – I know that Cassandra is fated to die.

Cease contention; draw no sword.

He held the gun on both of the culprits, though he knew that there was – probably – only one. The bag of cash was on the sidewalk. He wondered what he should do if the one who was the culprit – or both of them, if there were two – decided to grab the bag of cash and run away. He was hoping that the police would soon arrive.

Chapter 6
Apollo 3

A bad time for you to come, John, sighs Apollo. It is turning out to be a stressful day. Achilles and Hector were fighting fiercely. At first the two warriors were as two trees that grew for centuries – competing for the sunshine in each other's shade. But then, Achilles managed to land a fatal blow. Hector fell to his knees and choked up blood. His body is now lying there, on the field. Do you see what I find so distressful? Achilles is tying Hector's corpse to his chariot. His lips are grim and fire is blazing in his eyes. Come closer, so you get a better view.

Throw reins on thy passions.

Your body – such as it is – is proof against my sword, John, but there is a weakness in your armour nevertheless. Just stand there frowning earnestly while I show you why you must yield. The sharpest blades, John, have always been the great truths. You are an amateur in the field of combative ideas. What you don't seem quite able to grasp, my friend, is that the gods are human constructs – myths – that depend on human creation and belief for their continuance. They are embodiments – concrete images – of the forces that the humans see as at work in their lives. When humans change, their views of some of these forces will change – their view of war, for instance – and there will be no more human need for such gods as the god of war.

Her towers from all their heights pull down.

Oh it's fine to sacrifice to the gods, John – there's no harm in that at all – the gods might send a favourable wind or a sunny hour – but the humans shouldn't fool themselves into thinking that the gods invented such detriments as famine and cruelty and war. Those are human constructs, my friend – as human as the gods that the humans have made. Take a climb up Mount Olympus – you won't find anything but rock. The gods are all in the mind of the human race. We gods are human-gods, John – just as much as is human-peace or human-war.

I'll just use abstract words

A god who is having a stressful day.
A person who expects a perfect life.
The altering of one's DNA.

he thought

Do you watch the nightly news?
Want to know what's going on?
What is happening on the other side of the world?

as I have no images.

It is not a conception of intellect.
It is not a conception of prose.
It is a conception nearer to music than anything else.

He lacked the strength to carry the sack of grain to the mill. He had no bread to eat as the cupboard was completely bare.
These works seem too full of death.
Of course we gods – the recipients of sacrifice and prayer – were never meant to be a religion, John. The humans who told our stories knew that we were fiction – the stuff of a series of tales. They thought us up while trading yarns around the fires. They imagined us as entities that would embody the forces that they saw in their lives – in their own human lives. It was as if – they thought – some human-resembling creatures, with super-human powers, were operating by a combination of logic and whim – of thought and of emotion – each one vying for control in every situation in which you humans were competing among yourselves. Yes, you humans, John, you humans – I have decided that you are a human, after all. What gives you away is your compassion. Cassandra couldn't draw one tear – with her petty, little, pity-me, human-story – from among the whole panoply of gods. We gods accept things as they are, John – unlike you humans who cry so self-pityingly as your tears run down your cheeks and make little, tiny dents in the blood-soaked ground.
To live in thrall to so stern a fate.
You are on your knees and sagging, John – there is blood at the corner of your mouth. In the dust lies what you thought was your idea-sword. Yes, John – yes – this is disturbing, no doubt, to hear, but my words – my fine-honed words – are the painful truth. They are the spear that is piercing that gleaming armour that you so smugly wear, as you strut between the humans and the gods. I am a creation of the humans – of which you, John, are one – and so I and all of the gods on Mount Olympus are only here because you humans put us here. We represent the forces that you humans see in life. We have been created by you humans and we will not go away until you humans think of

some other – more pertinent – more relevant – myth to spin as you sit and philosophize around the fire.

Helen was written about by many classical authors. She was a character in many an epic poem. She was known to Homer and known to Virgil. Known to Cicero and Aristophanes. Every author made the Helen-story his own.

Helen standing on the deck and looking outward. The slapping of the waves and the snapping of the sail. Somewhere on the sea between Sparta and Troy. How did I become the topic of such contention? How did Paris talk me into sailing away?

Watching the battle of Hector and Achilles with Apollo.
Almost as if we're watching a televised game.

I am an egg lying on a beach! Soon I will be born! I can hear the sounds of a feast!

Accompanied by magnanimity - it might never out - make sense of the gossip - believe what she says - each hit by an arrow - a perfectly innocent person - head for home - take care to never forget - your life is a bauble - lava-spewing shocks.

"O friends," said stern Achilles, "now that the gods have brought this man thus down, I'll freely say, he brought more bane to Greece than all his aiders. Try we then, thus arm'd at ev'ry piece, and girding all Troy with our host, if now their hearts will leave their city clear, her clear stay slain, and all their lives receive, or hold yet, Hector being no more. But why use I a word of any act but what concerns my friend, Patroclus? Dead, undeplor'd, unsepulchred, he lies at fleet, unthought on! Never hour shall make his dead state, while the quick enjoys me, and this pow'r to move these movers. Though in hell, men say, that such as die Oblivion seizeth, yet in hell in me shall Memory hold all her forms still of my friend.

Now, youths of Greece, to fleet bear we this body of Patroclus, pæans sing, and all our navy greet with endless honour; we have slain Hector, the period of all Troy's glory, to whose worth all vow'd as to a god." This said, a work not worthy him he set to; of both feet Achilles bor'd the nerves through from the heel to th' ankle, and then knit both to his chariot with a thong of whitleather, his head trailing the centre.

The axle is
above the mud.

I have never had to shoulder such a burden, John, sighs Apollo. Never a task has drawn so heavily on my mind. It is taking all my powers of concentration. I put my fingers on my temples and focus my eyes. See there? – the body of Hector? – see it dragged around the field? – see the chariot of Achilles churning up the dust? Please don't speak, as I want to give it my full attention. I must bend each nerve and synapse in Hector's aid. It is all I can do to protect his body from being damaged. How I wish that I had more power than I have.

This wrong had been the last foul thing.

Your countenance has sagged a trifle, John. Your hurricane is now a gentle breeze. Your self-assurance a ragged morsel for the dogs and the fowl. So sorry to disabuse you, my friend, but isn't it better for you – the great truth-teller – to acknowledge that you and your fellow-humans are the source of all this grief and all this pain? It is not we gods who desire destruction, John – it is you humans who rule the earth. We gods simply embody the forces – light and dark – that you humans see in your own deepest selves. We destroy because you destroy – we sometimes relent because you relent. The sizes and proportions – of good and of harm – of building up and smashing down – might seem outsized to you, but these elements in our makeup are projections of human desires. You humans wish to have more power – for kindness and for cruelty – than you actually do.

"Russian President Putin repeated his position that NATO expansion to include Ukraine was unacceptable. President Putin warned other countries that any attempt to interfere with the Russian action would lead to 'consequences they have never seen'."

There will be creatures
lucky and unlucky
thought the rain.

I am an egg lying on a beach! Soon I will be born! I can hear the sounds of a battle!

Should the heart be filled
with blood?,
or should the mind be filled
with light?,
wondered the Being.

Apollo's lips curled into a smile. Of course, he could not take back a power. But he could give another one. He would curse the girl, Cassandra. From now on, nothing that she predicted would be believed.

Cassandra could find no receptive ears. If she said the jug was empty everyone believed it full. If she said that it would rain they stayed outdoors. They grew angry at her predictions, though never would they believe. Everyone told her they preferred her lips be sealed.

"The outcome of the war, many commentators have come to believe, might well be determined by the future actions of one man. We have learned that the great Achaean warrior, Achilles, is reconsidering his role in the war, as he has been inactive in the fighting so far. Apparently, the death of his friend and fellow-warrior, Patroclus, is an event which has caused him – Achilles – to reconsider and re-evaluate his status, vis a vis his participation in the battles that undoubtedly lie ahead in this great confrontation between two well-armed and very determined foes."

Neither piety nor wisdom protects against fate.
There is beauty and dignity in human life.
To have been a great soul is everything.

He took a stick and drew a diagram in the dirt. It showed how a sack of bread could be taken to turn into grain at the mill.

T'is a task too dangerous to take part.

So think about it, John – face a smidgin of the truth. What if peace were to break out in Troy? – what if the two sides should lay down their spears and have a joint-feast? Would that mean no more wars? Would that mean no more gods who have the relentlessly-human desire to tear things down? To shed blood – whether innocent or not – whether of warrior or of child? – whether of queen or of needed mother of infant babe? We gods will be here as long as humans inhabit the earth, John. And we will be human in all the ways – human and inhuman – that humans think and feel, and in all the vicious things that humans do.

Those friends thou seek'st are slain.

So go back to your human world, John. Tell them the gods are as real as are you – because they are made of the same swamp of grey-matter that festers between your ears. Because they are made of the same sack of throbbing gristle that pumps your fetid blood. Because they are made with the same grim hands that rape the mother and slash the throat of the new-born child. Tell all that to your high-minded humans and see what they say.

Andromache pricks her finger. She hears a shriek of great alarm. She knows the voice but wonders what the alarm could mean. It came from up in the tower. I know that voice as well as my own. For sure it's the terrified voice of the Queen.

Andromache on the walls of Troy. Looking down as a chariot churns up the dust. Peering through the dust as the chariot turns and approaches the Trojan walls. Every eye is on Andromache – no voice on the parapet speaks a word. She crumples and her forehead bloodies the wall.

So what does Apollo want from me, I wonder.

A smear of the balm of human-compassion to ease his plight.

I am an egg lying on a beach! I am ready to be born! I will eat with my fingers or thrust with my spear!

It was as clear - outshin'd the blaze of fire - who owns a story - my way of reminding - on and off the stage - as clearly as i can - he kept forgetting - my power is unlimited - something with substance - jaws of a deadly embrace.

Up he got to chariot, where he laid the arms repurchas'd, and scourg'd on his horse that freely flew. A whirlwind made of startled dust drave with them as they drew, with which were all his black-brown curls knotted in heaps and fil'd. And there lay Troy's late gracious, by Jupiter exil'd to all disgrace in his own land, and by his parents seen; when, like her son's head, all with dust Troy's miserable queen, Hecuba, distain'd her temples, plucking off her hon-our'd hair, and tore her royal garments, shrieking out.

In like kind Priam bore his sacred person, like a wretch that never saw good day, broken with outcries. About both the people prostrate lay, held down with clamour; all the town veil'd with a cloud of tears. Ilion, with all his tops on fire, and all the massacres, left for the Greeks, could put on looks of no more overthrow than now fraid life.

That was the year
that the river rose.

This is the end, John, sighs Apollo. If not the end, at least the beginning of the end. I can protect Hector's body, if I concentrate with every fibre of my being – if I summon up all the power at my command. See! – see the body as it is dragged by Achilles's chariot! It bounces on the ruts and is covered in dust! But look closely – look at the head – look at the face. Not a mark! – not a cut! – not a scrape! No broken bones – no signs of anguish on his countenance. But this is only by way of compensation. There are larger issues here, as you can imagine. A huge rock is rolling down a mountain – there is no way I can roll it back to an earlier time. In my foolishness, I tipped the scales of contention. It is a sad god you find here today, John. I lack the power to prevent the fall of Troy.

This never again shall bear green leaves or branches.

You have nothing to gain, Apollo, by any further cruelty. You are adding nothing positive to the ongoing life and legacy of humankind. You would ap-pear in a brighter light if you were to make a magnanimous gesture and release the girl from this heinous, unrelenting, oppressive curse.

Actual life becomes a story when ambered by a voice.

As sure as the sun, the moon and the stars,

A feast of imagery.
A pool of blood on a palace floor.
A god who does not control the future.

the Achaeans will fail,

Is the world a ball of shining promises?
Trembling in every threatening breeze from the open window?
Threatening to fall and smash to pieces on the floor?

hissed the other.

I would be strong, he thought, if I could eat some of the bread that I would be about to carry in a sack to the mill. If only I were a god, he thought, and had the power to take a stick and draw in the dirt and re-design the functioning of the world.

No prayers shall ever breed affection in me.

Nobody crosses me, John, and gets away with it – do you understand? At least those over whom I have control. Some of the gods have done me wrong – I've a memory which doesn't forget. I'll take my anger out on anyone I can. Wrong has been done to me, my friend. Wrong that I – at the time – was helpless to prevent, and since that time I've been helpless to avenge. This girl for whom you are whining – begging and pleading and snivelling – grovelling, to your everlasting shame – is simply going to have to pay the price.

I hope my own strength is not lost.

So – do I tell Cassandra that Apollo might listen? – that he might relieve the curse? Do I pretend I don't know what will happen? – conceal the history that I know, and base our whole relationship on a sentimental lie? Life was simpler when I had no crystal-ball.

Chapter 7
Cassandra 3

I'm on a ship, somewhere at sea, John, Cassandra is saying. You know of Agamemnon, I assume. A big wave smacks the prow as he sits on his wobbly captain's chair – which he insists on referring to as his regal throne. He acts so solemn as the ship bobs up and down. He is taking me back to Argos as his slave, as I well know – but he is trying to convince me that I will be his new queen. His wife is Clytemnestra, he is saying. He professes to have become quite enamoured of me. He wants me to rule beside him – share his kingdom and all he commands. What will your wife do while I am ruling?, I ask him, over and over again. Is there room enough for two on her queenly throne?

Thou tormen'st thy vex'd mind.

Oh why have you come back, John? Do you enjoy bringing terrible news? At least Apollo is indifferent. He lets me suffer without his presence. He doesn't watch me writhe and squirm. You know – your friendship brings almost as much pain as Apollo's enmity. You know what I go through and yet you do nothing to alleviate my burden. I assume you only come back to see me tortured before your eyes. The kind of friend whose heart rises up as mine sinks down.

Words like Fate

A girl who is a prisoner on a ship at sea.
Birds floating down a river.
A peasant who yearns for bread to eat.

and Necessity

Do you see images as palaces?
Dining halls and ancestral trophies?
A large safe with all the family plate and jewels?

and Will.

Wisdom is knowing what you are.
Wisdom is knowing your place in the world.
Reverence and a sense of proportion are what one needs.

You are as cruel, John, as is Apollo, as you know the agony that I go through and yet you refuse – time after time – to act on my behalf. You profess to offer sympathy, but you leave and come back with empty hands. Your heart is a fistful of ice – the frozen flint of a mountain pass. You look on cruelty in the extreme and are not moved. Perhaps if Apollo could see me suffer – as you can see me now – he would relent and lift the burden and bring me more comfort than I have ever gotten from you.
All that day even till the sun went down.
He was lost deep in the woods. Others had been there before him.

Helen sitting on the wall and looking in the distance. Going over the events that have brought her, here, to Troy. Becoming aware of the consternation down in the courtyard. Another messenger with word from far away. How did I become the cause of all this pain?
Helen's story was a story that was always welcome. There were those who knew the story in great detail. It was a story that was told at many a fire. The mothers would caution their husbands as they put a log on the ashes. Save her story until the children have gone to bed.

Suppose I were to appear to Agamemnon.
Wondering what Agamemnon would have to say.

Too soon the time
to see the whole picture.
Too muddy the water
to see the entire depth.

Images as friends - a bargaining chip - adding nothing positive - as two trees - every level of the mind - a stimulus to thought - read this action truly - my powers of discernment - the nature of the world - seems to be your mission.

When those in siege before the town so strange an uproar heard, behind, amongst their flocks and herds (being then in council set) they then start up, took horse, and soon their subtle enemy met, fought with them on the river's shore, where both gave mutual blows with well-pil'd darts. Amongst them all perverse Contention rose, amongst them Tumult was enrag'd, amongst them ruinous Fate had her red-finger; some they took in an unhurt estate, some hurt yet living, some quite slain, and those they tugg'd to them by both the feet, stripp'd off and took their weeds, with all the stream of blood upon them that their steels had manfully let out. They far'd as men alive indeed drew dead indeed about.

To these the fi'ry Artizan did add a new-ear'd field, large and thrice plough'd, the soil being soft, and of a wealthy yield; and many men at plough he made, that drave earth here and there, and turn'd up stitches orderly; at whose end when they were, a fellow ever gave their hands full cups of luscious wine; which emptied, for another stitch, the earth they undermine, and long till th' utmost bound be reach'd of all the ample close. The soil turn'd up behind the plough, all black like earth arose, though forg'd of nothing else but gold, and lay in show as light as if it had been plough'd indeed, miraculous to sight.

The wheel is
below the axle.

Come and look at this now, John. Cassandra is beckoning me. I am on deck somewhere at sea, she is saying. I am cringing against the gunwale. Two snakes crawl along the deck as I wriggle away. I faint, as if in a trance. See – my stomach rises and falls. My body lies prone – I toss and turn, as if in a dream. The snakes approach my ears – one on either side of my head. They rise and flick their tongues. Apollo's snakes have found me again. The snakes are whispering another prediction in my ears.

Only Zeus sweet slumber seized not.

Oh I am bitter, John. I am disillusioned – I am disappointed in you. I had hopes that you were a new kind of being. A being who had power to intervene with the gods. Who would bring empathy and kindness to Mount Olympus. Who would open the heads of the gods and pour therein a full measure of compassionate ideas. Bring them gently to a knowledge of what it is like to be a human. Cause them to rededicate their powers to easing the burden of the living of these tragically-human lives. End the wars – ease the suffering – do away with the loss and the heartbreak and the strife.

"'President Putin has chosen a premeditated war that will bring a catastrophic loss of life and human suffering,' said American President Joe Biden. 'Russia alone is responsible for the death and destruction that this attack will bring, and the United States and its Allies and partners will respond in a united and decisive way.'"

There will be creatures
who will survive and who will perish
thought the magma.

I could ask Apollo to solve the problems of plastics in the ocean and genocide and flooding and wildfires and the diminishing of wildlife habitat.

I have only just begun
and already
I am forced to compromise.
Perhaps this entity
will be more trouble
that it is worth.

She told them a story of great destruction. Of offense to the gods and of turmoil to those of the earth. Of the shifting of the foundations of the city. Of the crumbling of the columns and the beams. She told them that Troy would fall as sure as would fall the rain.

What could Cassandra gain, they wondered, by telling such a story. What earthly advantage would spur her to tell such a lie. They applied the deepest wisdom of the moment. They dismissed her story as having no human logic. They dismissed her story as having no value at all.

"It is believed that Hector, the great Trojan leader, met with his wife and child – some feel for the last time. Our sources report that she pleaded with him to stay within the walls of Troy and not return to the battlefield. Hector, true to form, our sources say, refused to listen to her advice and will return to the scene of battle at a strategic but undisclosed time."

Human life is always dramatic.
Human concerns are always in play.
No separation of public and private themes.

You were my hope for a change, John – neither a human nor a god. Now I see you are just a human after all. Oh John, you seemed to be so compassion-ate – I prayed that you were what you seemed to be. And yet, I see, now, that you can't – or won't – do anything to relieve this curse that is hanging over my head – this cloud that rains down blood on all who dwell within the environs of my person. I am not only the bearer of misery, John, I am the cause of all the misery in other's lives. Oh don't see me as simply Cassandra – my life is not what this is about – I represent the accumulated misery of all our kind. You are a human – you are a human – that's what you have told me again and again. Well see me, then, as the human of humans – the repository of all the accumulated misery of all the people who are cursed to live on this earth, with all the weight of the blood-soaked centuries crushing them down. Your visit has been such a failure – you were my final, faintest hope. If your presence is not the answer, John, then I see no hope at all for humankind.
He threw his sceptre against the ground.
He was lost deep in the woods. Others had been there before him. Many had come back. The lost had taken their axes and made a mark on the bark. All

he had to do was to follow the blazed trail.

Andromache in the bedroom of the palace. Slabs of oak stand guard at the entrance. Achaeans shouting and hacking with their swords. Someone calls for a battering ram. Clutching her son and instructing the maids to stand back from the door.

Andromache clutching her son to her bosom. They are throwing the male children from the city walls. She stands in a group of women and children. A gang of rough Achaeans looks her over. They refer to the boy as 'Hector's son'.

Maybe Agamemnon sees himself as another Paris.
Shaking the roots of a kingdom for love of a girl.

Strum without words
until you have them.
Surely this story
will make some sense.

A tale of Apollo and his human.
A tale of Cassandra and her god.

Dust settles - point out the paths - the gods disagree - blood through a vein - helpless to prevent - hid in eternal snow - all the massacres - soothes his bloody vein - first among the gods - in some unfathomable way.

There grew by this a field of corn, high, ripe, where reapers wrought, and let thick handfuls fall to earth, for which some bought bands, and made sheaves. Three binders stood, and took the handfuls reap'd from boys that gather'd quickly up, and by them armfuls heap'd. Amongst these at furrow's end, the King stood pleas'd at heart, said no word, but his sceptre show'd. And from him, much apart, his harvest-bailiffs underneath an oak a feast prepar'd and having kill'd a mighty ox, stood there to see him shar'd which women for their harvest folks (then come to sup) had dress'd, and many white wheat-cakes bestow'd, to make it up a feast.

He set near this a vine of gold, that crack'd beneath the weight of bunches black with being ripe; to keep which at the height, a silver rail ran all along, and round about it flow'd an azure moat, and to this guard, a quickset was be-stow'd of tin, one only path to all, by which the pressmen came in time of vin-tage. Youths and maids, that bore not yet the flame of manly Hymen, baskets bore, of grapes and mellow fruit. A lad that sweetly touch'd a harp, to which his voice did suit, center'd the circles of that youth, all whose skill could not do the wanton's pleasure to their minds, that danc'd, sung, whistled too.

*It crested the banks
of the river in Hades.*

Watch him try to hold my hand, John, as he points at the spit of land – Agamemnon, the amorous warrior-conqueror king. He wants to hold my hand as we enter the harbour at Argos. So many years he has been away. He tells me his feelings are not the same. He tells me that his wife won't be the woman he wooed and wed. He finds that I am the mate of his soul, though he has no idea of the voices that are hissing inside my head. If he knew of my prediction – what the snakes have imparted to me – well, it wouldn't make any difference, John. He would be like everyone else – he would smile and say what all the others say. That my mind is overactive – that things will turn out right in the end. He expects to live out his years – in the bosom of his kingdom – in marital joy – with Clytemnestra waiting, as a servant, I assume, on me.

Our Greek earth shall be drown'd in just tears.

I am sorry that you have been offered no relief. I have asked, repeatedly, Cassandra, for a reprieve on your behalf. Perhaps if I try, just one more time, it will make a difference.

This means that the story is fixed in time.

The only thing that was agreed was that the two snakes –

*A letter which might remain unread.
A god who is busy watching a war.
Birds caught captive in a mesh.*

whatever the message –

Do you see images as castles?
Stout walls and a deep moat?
With bombardment as a daily enterprise?

would speak with one voice.

Suppose I insist that I'm from a future country? I tried to tell Cassandra at first, but she didn't believe me. Each time I mentioned 'Canada', the words that followed failed, somehow, to be perceived as anything more than a string of meaningless sounds. Suppose I insist on what I tried to tell her earlier – that she is a character in books that I have read? She thinks that she is real – she *is* real, of course – I'm sure she'll insist that she is – but I'll insist that yes, she *is* real – yes, she is *certainly* real for sure – but not in the same way – not in quite the same way – as am I. But in whatever form of real – real-for-her or real-for-me – for neither Cassandra nor for Apollo can the future be changed in any significant way.

A man like heaven's immortals form'd.

He was lost deep in the woods. Others had been there before him. Many had come back. The lost had taken their axes and made a mark on the bark. All he had to do was to follow the blazed trail. But – when he looked, every single tree in the forest had been blazed.

45

Chapter 8
Apollo 4

Apollo is sulking in his tent. Go away, John! – please go away! Perhaps we are somewhere on Mount Olympus, but I can't be sure. It is a very large tent and I see no door. I am not at home today, John, Apollo is pleading. He is slumped on what I take to be his throne. There is trouble on his brow. There is pain in his eyes. He stares at the scattered armour that is strewn on the carpeted floor. A god who is trying to figure out where to go from here.

Yet even these counsels still would hear.

The gods seek balance, John, above all. We all sought to keep a balance in the Trojan War. Athena and Hera aided the Achaeans. Myself, my mother, Leto, even the great Zeus himself, all aided the Trojans. But we all had to live with a terrible, terrible thought. We all knew that Troy would fall and that we were helpless to prevent it. So when the final catastrophe happened, John, when the horse was left on the beach and the Achaeans breached the walls, well – human buildings were burned, and human lives were lost, and human agonies were multiplied like flies, of course – it was a terrible occurrence, gods and humans would all agree – but it was a shock with cosmic implications – a greater shock, John, than a human could possibly know.

The parted waves against her ribs did roar.

The fall of Troy reminded us, John, of a limit to our powers – that fall was a reminder to us of what we knew ourselves to be. We are as helpless, John, as humans. We are all Cassandras, John – we have terrifying knowledge, but we have not been entrusted with the gift of transformative power. We live with this knowledge in the depths of our minds, but on the surface of our minds, we live – and act – with the illusion that we are in charge. Humans do good and humans do harm, John, gods do good and harm as well, but there is a force – far above us – that governs outcomes that we can neither know nor understand. Limited power means that one has no power at all. And this is the primal curse, John – a curse for humans, of course, but you'd see it as a far greater curse if you were a god.

The only images

A god who is sulking in his tent.
Looking back through some notebooks.
A hope for a new kind of being.

that I can think of

How many wrongs are there in the world?
How many of these wrongs could you put right?
If you rolled up your sleeves and waded in?

are of the human.

Two sorrows are given for every blessing.
Whether by human action or by the whim of the gods.
This is the framework within which human life must be lived.

Water has always flowed downhill, the wise man told him. It has been so from the beginning of things as they are.
Nor had they music less divine.
You are sulking in your tent. Your side has lost the Trojan War. Is empathy an attribute of the gods? Any remorse concerning the curse you placed on Cassandra? She is now an Achaean slave. She is predicting the fall of Agamemnon and her own demise. Perhaps a stay of execution? – if such is within your power? If it is, perhaps you'd like to change your mind. If events are out of your hands, then what of your feelings? Remorse? – reconciliation? – redemption? Any chance that you are yearning for any of these?

Helen making her way among the debris. Trying to make sense of the total destruction of Troy. Scorched timbers and broken bricks on the floor of the palace. Wondering who is now the vanquished and who is the victor. I wonder what will happen to me now?
So here's the mystery in the story of Helen. Was she a human who was creating her own story? Was she a plaything at the mercy of the gods? How to scrape away the husk of the story-tellers? How to know what she might have thought of it all herself?

Apollo – the god who blames the humans for what is wrong.
Apollo – who interferes in human lives and wars.

I am standing in front of a person! Another person is standing in front of me! We are talking about the nature of the world!

Find a cave - exhausted swimmers - a dramatic situation - at a lower depth - helpless to avenge - wavering like a sheep - trying to convince me - it is not known - a simple letter - there are forces.

"Rejoice," said Achilles, "O my Patroclus, thou courted by Dis now. Now I pay to thy late overthrow all my revenges vow'd before. Hector lies slaughter'd here dragg'd at my chariot, and our dogs shall all in pieces tear his hated limbs. Twelve Trojan youths, born of their noblest strains, I took alive; and, yet enrag'd, will empty all their veins of vital spirits, sacrific'd before thy heap of fire." This said, a work unworthy him he put upon his ire, and trampled Hector under foot at his friend's feet.

Rage varied Achilles's distraction; horse, chariot, in haste he call'd for; and, those join'd, the corpse was to his chariot tied, and thrice about the sepulchre he made his fury ride, dragging the person. All this past; in his pavilion rest seiz'd him, but with Hector's corpse his rage had never done, still suff'ring it t'oppress the dust. Apollo yet, ev'n dead, pitied the prince, and would not see inhuman tyranny fed with more pollution of his limbs; and therefore cover'd round his person with his golden shield, that rude dogs might not wound his manly lineaments, which threat Achilles cruelly had us'd in fury.

The wheel is
in the mud.

Leave us alone, please, John. We want our privacy, Apollo mumbles. Do you have no respect for the mother of a god? It is Leto – the mother of Apollo. She sits beside him and holds his hand. Leave this place – come back to Delos. It is anchored and secure. I will talk to Zeus and see what I can do. The other gods are wrong to blame you for the fall of Troy. It was fated, my son, by a far superior force, so the fall of Troy was nothing of your affair. Even Zeus has had no power to defy the Fates. Oh please, my son, do not give in to despair. Zeus will remind the other gods of the truth of the matter. Promise me that you will never blame yourself.

This man breaks all such bounds.

You humans! You humans! A curse upon you all! The wretchedness of my life is that I am patterned after you! Your flaws are my flaws! Your agonies are my agonies! Your mistakes are my mistakes! Your heartbreaks are my heartbreaks! I fell in love with a girl as humans fall in love! I was rejected as humans are rejected! I sought revenge as a human would seek revenge! The curse upon me is the curse upon you! I am made – John – in your image! I am you and you are me 'til the end of time!

" 'The world will hold Russia accountable,' said American President Biden shortly after Russian President Putin announced a further invasion of Ukraine and amid reports of bombs and artillery fire in several Ukrainian cities."

There will be creatures
who will survive and who will perish
thought the rain.

I am becoming another person! Another person is becoming me! We are talking about the nature of the world!

Let the heart be filled
with blood.
Let the mind be void
of light.

Cassandra told of confusion and distortion. Of the killing of a husband and a king. Of a pool of blood on a palace floor. Of a knife that would pierce the heart of a family. She said that Agamemnon would fall as sure as would fall the sun.

What could Cassandra gain, they wondered, by telling such a story. What earthly advantage would spur her to tell such a lie. They applied the deepest wisdom of the moment. They dismissed her story as having no human logic. They dismissed her story as having no value at all.

"It is not known, at this time – and perhaps will never be known – how much the gods have had a hand in the events here at Troy. So far, the course of the war seems to have been subject to a mixture of Free Will and what both sides are referring to as Fate, a very vaguely-defined word – a catchphrase, it would seem, without a definite meaning which all can agree upon. Clearly there are gods, of course – both sides attest to that – but what is not as clear, at this time, is the role of the gods in this whole destructive, interminable affair."

Passionate delight in the gifts that the living of life affords.
Apprehension at the dark framework that lingers and looms.
Tragedy is the tension between these two.

So he built his house and holdings on the top of a high hill. A tethered goat, some chickens, a shanty, and a wife and a son.
He never shall persuade at my hands.
Or is this the case, I wonder? Perhaps it is not – perhaps not at all! This – perhaps – is a double-curse – one bitter and one quite mild. The handle and the blade of the same sharp knife. Now that I think of it – looking at you, John – there is a difference in all of this. I am immortal and you are not! I will go on for thousands of years and you will die! You will cease to care while I will live on and on! The gods have been placed beneath the humans in terms of their allotments of terror and pain. I will live on beyond this Cassandra – beyond

Menelaus and his wandering wife – beyond Patroclus and Hector and Achilles and all the rest. Beyond you, John, and all you humans who cause such tiny, ant-like griefs in your own petty lives. This heart of mine will register shocks – searing, agonizing shocks, John – earth-shaking, lava-spewing shocks – for eons of time!

Andromache is not named in the scene with her husband. Perhaps the ancient singer forgot her name.

Andromache was known to her captors as 'Hector's wife'. That is the name by which she was bartered and sold.

Apollo – the god who falls prey to human emotions.
Apollo – who seeks revenge when human love is denied.

I am another person! Another person is me! We are talking about whether the nature of the world has changed!

The inner-drama - the other side of the world - carry great weight - the topic of our exchange - just not sure how - there is no doubt - buzzes with the news - a suggestion of endless depth - you are the only one - the kind of friend.

Shameless gods, authors of ill ye are to suffer ill. Hath Hector's life at all times show'd his care of all your rights, in burning thighs of beeves and goats to you, and are your cares no more of him? Vuchsafe ye not ev'n now, eve'n dead, to keep him, that his wife, his mother, and his son, father, and subjects, may be mov'd to those deeds he hath done, seeing you preserve him that serv'd you, and sending to their hands his person for the rites of fire?

Other men a greater loss than Achilles have undergone, a son, suppose, or brother of one womb; yet, after dues of woes and tears, they bury in his tomb all their deplorings. Fates have giv'n to all that are true men true manly patience; but this man so soothes his bloody vein that no blood serves it, he must have divine-soul'd Hector bound to his proud chariot, and danc'd in a most barbarous round about his lov'd friend's sepulchre, when he is slain. 'Tis vile, and draws no profit after it.

It wasn't rain
that swelled the river.

Apollo alone with his troubles. No – I would rather be alone, John, Apollo whimpers, as I stand here on the rug. I don't want anyone to bother me today. An immortal body – a spirit scorched – nothing seems to be going his way. Only time can heal such pain. Go back to where you came from, John – what are the gods and our troubles to you? I must calmly weigh my options – surely the Fates have relief in store – I am sure that all will turn out right in the end.

Apollo sulking in his tent. Caught between the higher powers and the humans. He slumps back on the throne and closes his eyes.

Far my free spirit is from serving thy command.

Remorse? – you want remorse? – reconciliation? – redemption? – all these shallow, petty, illogical, purely-human concerns? These are just thoughts, John, not facts. You think that stories all have endings – emotional baths that sooth the aches of mental sores – but every story is an ongoing saga – all the truths remain in place. Tomorrow the road will beckon – beckon and threaten with either hand. The rocks will be just as sharp as they are today. You have strayed from the path of inquiry to wander among the briars of emotional berry-picking – hoping to find a withered rose among the thorns.

The god an ill shaft spent.

Do you think that the gods are here solely to serve humankind? Do you think that we are the servants, and you are the gods? How can you have lived so many years and be so naive? Haven't you had your bumps and scrapes? Haven't you had wars in your time – and broken hearts and children falling and skinning their knees? Does the sun always shine where you come from? Sure, I have power over humans – I interfere in their lives all the time – but that they are perpetually happy is not my concern. Humans are expendable – John – have you not realized that? When one of them falls off a cliff, or tumbles into the dusty furrows, or bleeds to death on the battlefield, there are always more. Yes, certain gods have favourite humans – and we nurture them along, in our way – subject to the power of the other gods. I wanted to keep Cassandra safe and warm – but look what she has done – she turned against my gift! – she turned against me! And a god is never happy when being scorned. I am Apollo, the golden god. No one thwarts me and my will. No human will ever get the best of me. I will torment that girl until she lies in her grave.

I am disappointed in you – the great god, Apollo. You have undermined my sense of what it is to be a god. It has been painful to witness your petty approach to life.

The fierce dart did enter him beneath his ear, betwixt his jaw and it; drave down, cut through his tongue, and struck his teeth out.

Oh come on, John! – grow up! Face a fact or two for once! There are no gods! Get that through your head! We gods are a myth – a human construct – a product of the human imagination – a body of imagery in a pattern – which comes from the deepest level of the human mind – a pattern of images which seeks to embody – in concrete artistic form – the eternal human condition. Oh sure – we gods might pass away – if people cease to see us as a viable image-pattern – but there will be other myths constructed in the human mind. You can't get away from being human, John – which is essentially what you've been seeking – no matter how frantically you might try. You will be human – and think like a human – with all the agony and the ecstacy – the glory and the grime – and you will keep making myths – image-patterns of your concerns – 'til the end of time.

Unless another voice decides to re-tell the story.

I know a way of solving this problem,

A god stabbing a human in the back.
An attempt to become one's essential self.
A theme of profound tragedy.

hissed both snakes together,

How wide or narrow should be your focus?
Which is the wound that bleeds the most?
Should you dedicate your life to a single cause?

as if with one voice.

Then one spring the water rose halfway up the high hill. It threatened to inundate the man, the goat, the chickens, the shanty, the wife and the son.
Afford impression of it in thy soul.
John! John! John! Pity me! – Oh pity me! I am made in the image of the human! That makes me a tragic figure! Nothing I aspire to can ever be achieved! I fall on my face and slide back down as I approach the last few footsteps at the top of the hill! Yes, I see myself as tragic, John – as tragic as any human you can name! I tried to right the imbalance – to take the wobble out of the flight! But I couldn't erase the flaw – the flaw that lies at the heart of the universe! There's a lesson to my story, John! I have been made in the image of the human! I am an image – in larger dimensions – of humankind! And the human is the flaw at the heart of all things!
Sad subject of so hard a fate.
Cassandra doesn't believe me when I tell her that the reason why I believe her is that I came to her through the pages of a book – that she is trapped because she's a character in a myth. Of course, her belief in my story – her acceptance of the truth of what I say – whatever other effect it might have – would make no difference to the story that she finds herself – in her agony – living through. However, she might come to realize that her myth will be always be valid, even when the last human leaves for the moon. In their spacesuits, they'll be characters in the *Iliad,* and the *Odyssey,* too – they'll take their human nature with them wherever they go. So, I wonder – I can't help but wonder – if she should ever come to believe – would this be any compensation to her at all?

Chapter 9
Cassandra 4

Cassandra, the slave-girl. A spoil from the sack of Troy. Here at the royal palace with King and Queen. She knows everything about them. Sees the knives aimed at the backs – sees the snares for the unwary – knows that death is coming their way. Cassandra stands and watches – hears every word that the monarchs say. The wife welcomes her husband – she missed him while he was away. The husband greets his wife – he missed his kingdom and all he commands. After fighting so long on land and after voyaging through treacherous seas, it will be pleasant to be able to let down his guard and enjoy the peaceful rewards of a welcomed king.

Apollo there did touch his most sweet harp.

I knew you couldn't help me, John – whether you were a god in disguise or a human from some other part of the world. Oh I had a faint hope that you were a god-above-the-gods, but that only lasted for a fleeting split-second in time. I looked in your eyes and knew it couldn't possibly be true. Didn't you realize, when I was cross with you for not helping me, that it was frustration on my part and nothing more? I knew, all along, that there was nothing that you could do. Don't forget – I can see the future. I saw you coming back empty-handed before you came. In fact, when the snakes tried to tell me that your concern would be of no avail, I silenced them, and told them that I already knew. It's good to know, though, John, that you have tried. I saw you in Apollo's tent, asking him for a last-minute reprieve. Asking him if he felt remorse for what he had done.

Forces above the god-like humans,

A girl who tells the truth and is not believed.
Improving a rough draft.
A soldier giving instructions as he dies.

forces above the human-like gods,

Are image-patterns sometimes frail?
Fatal flaws within the works?
Do image-patterns sometimes undermine themselves?

are images in the unreachable depths of my mind.

Human life is forever hard.
There is folly and there is wisdom.
At times there is no place for either of these.

And I saw you afterwards, when you sat on a bench outside his tent – on a ledge of Mount Olympus – and wondered how you were going to tell me the news. You at table with no appetite for thought – Apollo's bloody answer on your platter – wordy spices failing to disguise the bitter truth. Surprised that I know? – I can see that you are, John – but I have known every thought that you have had in your head. I can not only see the future, I can hear what people are thinking. But I haven't needed special powers to know what you've thought – I have been reading your thoughts in your face all along. A compensation for me, John – after you talked to Apollo – as you sat there on the bench – were the tears that I saw in your eyes.
They sacrificed and cast the offal to the deeps.
Wisdom was all around them – a mist that hovered in the air.

Helen sitting and knitting by the fireplace. An old lady with a story she keeps to herself. Oh I am aware that I am the subject of constant gossip. No one on earth could possibly know what I think of myself. Sometimes I wish I could have stayed in the egg.

Cassandra – the painting on the vase on the palace mantle.
Cassandra – the broken, shattered vase on the palace floor.

A lyre bent and battered.
Rescued from the flames of Troy.
An old man strumming tentatively
seeking the words for an epic song.

Splendid in her own way - some of the elements - the world i live in - have no images - all gods seek balance - knowing what you are - the bottom of the ocean - strayed from the path - fixed in time - more a mask than a face.

A herd of oxen then he carv'd, with high rais'd heads, forg'd all of gold and tin, for colour mix'd, and bellowing from their stall rush'd to their pastures at a flood, that echo'd all their throats, exceeding swift, and full of reeds; and all in yellow coats four herdsmen follow'd; after whom, nine mastiffs went. In head of all the herd, upon a bull, that deadly bellowéd, two horrid lions rampt, and seiz'd, and tugg'd off bellowing still; both men and dogs came; yet they tore the hide, and lapp'd their fill of black blood, and the entrails ate. In vain the men assay'd to set their dogs on; none durst pinch, but cur-like stood and bay'd in both the faces of their kings, and all their onsets fled.

Then in a passing pleasant vale, the famous Artsman fed, upon a goodly pasture ground, rich flocks of white-fleec'd sheep, built stables, cottages, and cotes, that did the shepherds keep from wind and weather. Next to these, he cut a dancing place, all full of turnings, that was like the admirable maze for fair-hair'd Ariadne made, by cunning Dædalus; and in it youths and virgins danc'd, all young and beauteous, and glewéd in another's palms. Weeds that the wind did toss the virgins wore; the youths wov'n coats, that cast a faint dim gloss like that of oil. Fresh garlands too, the virgins' temples crown'd; the youths gilt swords wore at their thighs, with silver bawdrics bound.

The wheel is
above the axle.

Agamemnon has gone into the palace. Clytemnestra turns and leaves. Cassandra speaks to the people. She tells them what she knows – tells them the import of her dreams. Agamemnon will fall – he will lie in a pool of his blood. And she – herself – Cassandra, the slave-girl – will lie in a pool of her own. The people scoff and smile at Cassandra and shake their heads. What could a slave be expected to know? They know their queen has prepared a welcome – she has told them she loves their king. Cassandra insists that she knows the future, but nothing she tells them makes any sense. Go into the palace and accept the hospitality of the household – the loving Queen and the kindly King. May you live long and may you prosper. You should be grateful that you survived the destruction of Troy.

To heaven the thick fumes bore enwrapped savours.

Actually, John, you'd be interested to know – lest you feel too much a failure in your chosen task – your quest to right the wrongs done to myself, on behalf of all humankind – that the King, my father – King Priam – came back from the underworld and met with the god, Apollo, the other day. He was given safe passage to Mount Olympus by some other gods. He met with Apollo in his tent. He asked Apollo to release me – his daughter, his precious daughter – from this curse. He didn't need a cart or a mule. He said that he realized that human gold and human jewels would not be of any worth to a god, so he went there empty-handed. All he had with which to ransom me was a display of a father's love. Read the anguish, he said, that is written on my face.

"A Ukrainian commentator called the consequences for his country 'catastrophic', lamenting Ukraine's descent back toward 'the status of a colony in a new Russian empire.'"

The flowing magma
decided not to bury
the ocean.

I could ask Apollo to solve the problems of runaway inflation and the inequitable global economy and conglomerate financial greed and all the other problems of 2022.

Blood will not come down
from the sun.
From the sun will come
the light.

Troy fell – Cassandra had known. Agamemnon fell – Cassandra had known. She lost her city – she lost her family – she lost her life. Only one thing did the snakes not whisper – only one thing did she yearn to know. Why should such a curse distort and destroy her life?

"It is a matter of speculation, at this time, as to what the wooden horse is, or represents, or is meant to achieve. It has, apparently, been left on the beach and the Achaean ships – which have been stationed on that beach for as long as the war has been pursued – are not in evidence today, as, apparently, they have all put out to sea. The Trojans are, reportedly, holding talks concerning the horse – an intriguing creation – a mysterious object – a baffling conundrum – in an effort to determine what course of action the Trojans would be best, in the opinion of their leaders, to pursue."

There is joy in the breath of life.
There is joy in human accomplishment.
Both of these the wind will scatter as the leaf.

Apollo didn't bat an eyelash, John – he didn't pause and think at all. He returned my father his answer in a trice. The curse would not be lifted – and that was that. My father came to me, here in Argos – as Agamemnon breathed a sigh of relief at returning home safely from the war – and told me of Apollo's brutal news, though I knew, of course, before he arrived. One more incremental tightening of the noose.
Nor sees by present things the future.
Wisdom settled on the grass and on the trees.

Almost nothing can be said about the story of Andromache.

Cassandra – the girl in the firelit chanting of the epic poem.
Cassandra – the girl in the sunlit performance of the ancient play.

Only time can write these words for you.
Wisdom comes slowly if at all.
Sit beside the smoking ruins
and hope that the words will fall into place.

A tale of wisdom – a tale of madness.
A tale of glory – a tale of woe.
Clotho, Lachesis, Atropos – Earth, Air, Water, Fire.
Sometimes in league – sometimes opposed.
Sometime sunshine behind a cloud – sometimes rain.

A tale of Apollo and his human.
A tale of Cassandra and her god.

Forced them to acknowledge - hatching in your mind - the adverse part
denied - have rescued from the debris - should be your focus - it was as if - mul-
tiplied like flies - there's plenty here - rate thy price - the cause of all this pain.

Sometimes all wound close in a ring, to which as fast they spun as any
wheel a turner makes, being tried how it will run, while he is set; and out again,
as full of speed they wound, not one left fast, or breaking hands. A multitude
stood round, delighted with their nimble sport; to end which two begun, mids
all, a song, and turning sung the sports conclusión, all this he circled in the
shield, with pouring round about, in all his rage, the Ocean, that it might never
out.

This shield thus done, he forg'd for him, such curets as outshin'd the blaze
of fire. A helmet then (through which no steel could find forc'd passage) he
compos'd, whose hue a hundred colours took, and in the crest a plume of gold,
that each breath stirr'd, he stuck. All done, he all to Thetis brought, and held
all up to her. She took them all, and like t' the hawk, surnam'd the osspringer,
from Vulcan to her mighty son, with that so glorious show, stoop'd from the
steep Olympian hill, hid in eternal snow.

It was the blood
of the men who had died.

The doors of the palace swing open. Clytemnestra holds out her arms.
She beckons the people to see what she wants them to see. It's the body of
Agamemnon. It's the body of Cassandra as well. They are caught up in a mesh
like captive birds. They are lying on a royal, purple robe. Clytemnestra speaks

to her people. She has done what she must do. She has done the work of the gods. She has brought justice to her hearth. Her husband – her former husband – had done her wrong. He had sacrificed their daughter – smashed the shrines he found at Troy – brought this slave-girl as an intruder into their home. The people debate the rights and the wrongs with her. Cassandra lies on the floor. What is her role in this frightening drama? What is the lesson the people have learned? Are there forces looking down from up above?

How like waves ills follow ills.

A letter – a simple letter – the kind we have in the modern world. I sit and hold it in my lap. Cassandra pulled it out of her smock and slipped it into my hand as she turned from the crowd and moved towards the palace-doors. I looked towards the crowd but, instantly, I remembered that they couldn't see me. They had no idea that Cassandra had spoken to me. So here I am in the city of Argos, in the busy marketplace, sitting on a bench as the city buzzes with the news. Chatter of Agamemnon, no doubt, of Clytemnestra and Aegisthus and of the slave-girl who was also murdered, though many of them wouldn't know her name. I can hear them, but I can't understand them – it is all Greek to me. If I want to know what they're saying, I can read a Greek play. In English translation, of course, as I don't know ancient or modern Greek – not a single word.

Then the first story begets a second story.

But we'll have to wait

Two cities fashioned on a shield.
The contemplation of a double-curse.
A god who is in a bind.

for a human

Do image-patterns sometimes totter?
Do image-patterns sometimes fall?
Do images in patterns come crashing down?

to come along.

Should I open up the letter? – would she have written in English to me? Perhaps she's already seen me open it – or do I have such a choice? If it's in Greek I won't have any idea what it says. To me, her death was an ending. Why would I want to open this letter? – why would she think that there would be anything more to say?

The other gods in all night slumber slept.
They had lungs that filtered the wisdom as they breathed.

No more with any god will I change lances.

John-Cassandra or John-Apollo? What to tell and what not to tell? What can be heard and what will be blown away on the breeze? Dozens of questions will cling like burrs when the story is stabled and eating its oats. I seem to have tumbled into a murky myth of my own. I try to climb out but slide back down on the slippery sides. But here's a desperate thought – a drop of water in the canteen – a sliver of sunlight in the cave on the mountain-side. Perhaps the labyrinth has an egress after all. If I am living in a dream, it means that, eventually, I'm bound to wake up. If it is a dream – or a nightmare, as this one seems to be – and I wake up and blink at the sunrise, it means that such questions will fade away, and I can shrug my shoulders and wipe the sleep from my eyes, and enjoy the realization – the reassurance – the knowledge – the belief – that these are questions about which I will never have to decide.

Chapter 10
John 2

Sitting in my car beside the river. Managed to make a few improvements to the rough draft. *Shakespeare and Cleopatra*. Started out as just an idea. It's nice when a novel wants to be written. It doesn't rest until it's found its ideal form.

Injustices being never so secure in present times.

I wonder what it is about Cassandra. Minding her own business – floating by in front of my eyes. The idea of Cassandra and her snakes won't let me alone.

Images elude me

A writer making improvements in a rough draft.
A wife pleading with her husband.
A girl who is a bargaining chip in a war.

as I seek for them

Do you see yourself as on a journey?
Or simply sitting in a rocking chair?
Does life fly by, overhead, above the clouds?

in vain.

All actions have their consequences.
Even the gods are not truly free.
To Necessity even the greatest of gods must bow.

The birds just flow with the current. No way of knowing if it's the same birds, though you could tag them if you wanted the truth to be known. And there's fish-finders now that can tell you what's below.

After-plagues even they are seen as sure.

How many chapters would I give to Cassandra? How many chapters would I give to Apollo? How many other characters would I include as well? How to get myself into their midst? Perhaps the best way to start – and to end – is 'en media res'. One of those stories that has no beginning and has no end.

So who, now, owns the story of Helen? Hers is a story that is made of putty or clay. A writer can mold it into any shape or form. It belongs to all the future Homers and Virgils. Underneath the ink they'll be writing about themselves.

Sitting in my car beside the river.
Always the chance that I will find some better words.

Dust settles
over everything.

In justest sort - most people would agree - forming intricate patterns - in lovely circles danc'd - i had a faint hope - judge by human terms - the primal curse - the image of the human - tumult was enrag'd - just as i planned.

The mud is above
the axle and the wheel.

There's also *Agamemnon*. Funny I haven't been thinking of that. There probably more Cassandra there than in the *Iliad*. Of course the question is how much Cassandra there is in me.
We asked a prophet that well knew the cause of all.
I sense that this would make a good novel – but it's hard to be sure. The nature of the universe – individuals caught in the maelstrom – some characters getting a fair shake and some of them not. Or – maybe it would be too contemporary – perhaps I'm too concerned with the news – all the things that are going on, at present, in the social world. A loud-hailer for all the injustices of the day. Literature as polemic – literature as a grab-bag of gripes. Just a shouted rant on my part – all the things that displease me under the moon and the sun. A novel with shallow characters – each expecting a perfect life. An arrogant male bray on the part of Apollo – all disdain and superiority and 'this is the way it is and I won't let go'. And an 'I-am-a-victim' mousy-squeal from Cassandra – 'caught in jaws that won't let me be my essential self'. Just a waste-basket full of stereotypes and clichés.

Over passions
of the moment
most of all.

The falling rain
decided not to cover
the land.

Passions flare up
with a temperature
as hot as the gasses
that fuel the sun.

I will poke two holes
in the cranium.
Let the light come –
or not come –
through the eyes.

What is it, then, to be mortal? What is it, then, to live and to breathe? Why this cycle of human suffering? A world in agony? – a world in flames? Why does sunshine only last until it rains?

And then they cool
as the fading day
brings shade.

Tune the string while the tempest blows.
Tune the string while the day is calm.
Seek always the truest, clearest note.

My coffee is almost gone. I always like to save some for the road. I should pack up my things and head for home. Put the new changes into the computer and print it again.
Scale Olympus and implore Zeus.
So – perhaps I should let it go. I have plenty of other novel-topics on my plate. I should look back through my notebooks and see what's there. Something with substance – something with relevance – something with bite.

The story of Andromache can barely be told.

Putting my pen and novel aside and driving home.
Cassandra sitting beside me as I drive.

Time passes
and dust settles
over all.

The urge to explore - i knew all along - all the business was - all their hopes - i am an image - the topic of such contention - let's be blunt - above the clouds - a curse for humans - all the stream of blood.

Exhausted swimmers
waved away the rescue boat.

Driving along the country roads. The sunlight sparkling on the snow. Who wouldn't want to live here, I always say. Draining the last drops of coffee from the cup. Soon be home and then I can get right back to work. Put these changes in the computer and print a new draft.

The heaven-hous'd gods are now indifferent grown.

Fair is Fair would have made a good title, though. A suggestion of endless depths if the reader would stick a big toe in the inky pool. Well, there's plenty of other topics and other titles will surely occur.

Then the second story is also fixed in time.

The two snakes watched

Claims that are dismissed as propaganda.
An egg lying on a beach.
A topic which is of very little concern.

as the coin flipped end over end

And what about your own life?
Do you think about it from time to time?
What conclusions have you come to – if any at all?

through the air.

Turning into the driveway. A very enjoyable coffee-drive. Put the garbage cans away and check for mail. A few more weeks and I'll send this novel on its way.

Of this tell Zeus, embrace his knee, and pray.

Why do I cling to Cassandra? – why does Cassandra cling to me? I'd say there's plenty here for a novel, what with the sources and the ideas. But – when would I fit it into my schedule? I have dozens of ideas for novels – I have ideas coming out of my ears. I can't let them just fall by the wayside. Who knows? – maybe Cassandra won't get to be a novel at all.

Cassandra

The Untold Story

A Poem by John-the-Character

1

Homer sat amid the destruction.
He sang as he strummed on his lyre.
Troy was still burning as he was chanting.
He could still hear the sound of the fire.

2

Falling from a great height always makes a great tale.
Homer was intrigued by the story of a young girl
Who found it difficult to live in this treacherous world.
Born a princess – she died a slave on foreign soil.

3

Cassandra ran afoul of Apollo.
He was in an ugly mood.
He placed a curse upon her
And disaster then ensued.

4

Cassandra was given to know the Future.
What she saw was quite appalling.
The Trojan city was on fire
And the Walls of the City were falling.

5

The Curse was like an ague –
It was like boils upon her head.
Before the story was over
Cassandra would be dead.

6

However – no need to repeat the story –
The story that Homer told so well.
Now can be told The Story
That Homer Didn't Tell.

7

Homer told the story
Of Apollo and His Curse.
But the part that Homer didn't tell
Is far, far worse.

8

Yes – the story that can now be told –
That Homer didn't tell –
Is that Cassandra could not only see the Future –
She could see the Past as well.

9

Yes – Homer told the story
Of Curse One and Curse Two,
But he was silent on Curse Three.
Perhaps he never knew.

10

Curse One was To Know the Future.
This vision caused Cassandra great pain.
The Second Curse was that No One Would Believe Her.
They turned their backs when she would explain.

11

Of the Third Curse, Homer is silent –
Not one word did he put into rhyme –
That Cassandra could See the Universe
From The Beginning to The End of Time.

12

The curse that Homer didn't mention –
The curse that he didn't put into verse –
Is that she could See Creation
From the Moment of its Birth.

13

Since no one would believe her –
They laughed when she said that Troy would fall –
She remained silent about Creation.
She didn't mention the topic at all.

14

It is not known how she traveled
To witness the very First Day.
Santa would probably not have taken her
To view it from his sleigh.

15

Santa once told a Human –
While on a ride –
That creatures from separate myths
Do not confide.

16

To Mythical Creatures – he said –
The other myths are known;
However, they cannot alter myths
On their own.

17

So far no Human has added Santa –
In a tale of epic rhyme –
To the Story of Cassandra
And had them visit the Beginning of Time.

18

So – perhaps Cassandra flew on her own.
You might say that can't be right –
Because Cassandra was a Human –
Unaware of the Secrets of Flight.

19

Even Leonardo –
As brilliant as he was –
Could not overcome
The Physics Laws.

20

But – the Wright Brothers were Human –
Of course they were –
And their knowledge – though far in the Future –
Would have been available to her.

21

Since she could see into the Future –
Along with all that went before –
She could certainly have watched the Wrights
At work in their bicycle store.

22

Perhaps Cassandra built a conveyance
And went on time-travel flights
Long before the air plane
Was invented by the Wrights.

23

Yes – we Humans could have known
Everything there was to know.
Cassandra knew everything
And would gladly have told us so,

24

But the Humans of her time
Turned Cassandra away.
They refused to listen
To what she had to say,

25

So Cassandra turned her back
On the Human Race.
Around herself she grew
A protective carapace.

26

But Creation is not the Whole Story
Of what Cassandra knew.
Not only did she know the Past
She knew the Future too.

27

Cassandra could see far into the Future –
Far beyond the Trojan War –
To the day when the Universe might end
With the collapse of every star.

28

Far beyond what our telescopes have learned –
Far beyond what our space-probes know –
Far beyond the distance
That our rocket-ships can go.

29

Is the Universe a loop? – a sphere?
Where does it come from and where does it go?
Cassandra had the answers
That only God – if there is one – could know.

30

Did the Universe begin
With God's fingerprints in the clay?
Or with the Big Bang?
Cassandra was able to say.

31

If Cassandra had told
All of this before,
We wouldn't have needed Newton –
Or Einstein – or Bohr.

32

Will the Universe end
With a Cataclysmic Action?
Prognostications of the Future
Would have provided no attraction.

33

If Cassandra had talked,
A number of people would not have been famous.
Like – Rasputin – or Edgar Cayce –
Or – in particular – Nostradamus.

34

Cassandra could have spoken –
In Homeric verse –
Of the Beginning – and the End –
Of the Entire Universe.

35

Cassandra saw into the Future,
But she chose to remain silent,
So we don't know whether the Future
Will be peaceful or be violent.

36

The ability to see the Future
Might have left Cassandra aghast.
We assume that she was able to see
How long Creation would last.

37

Perhaps she shrank from the Future –
At the Horror of the Curse;
Perhaps she was forced to witness
The End of the Universe.

38

However, Cassandra felt quite threatened.
She heard some Trojans say
That she should be taken to the dungeon –
And locked forever away.

39

So – since the words of Cassandra
Were rejected – every one –
She never told anybody
How the Universe had Begun.

40

So – to this day we don't know
How the Earth was Created.
To ignorance of this knowledge
We Humans seem to be fated.

41

Nor do we know the Ending
Of the Universe at all.
We wonder if – like the walls of Troy –
The Universe will Fall.

42

No – she never told of the Future –
Of how we – sadly – might come to an end.
Perhaps – with Cassandra's input –
The Laws of Physics we Humans might bend.

43

What – we wonder – might be the Trojan Horse
That could bring the Universe down?
Could we learn to prevent The Implosion
So we'll always be around?

44

As we stumble into the Future
Without Cassandra's guidance
Will we suffer a Universal Doom
Or can we manage its avoidance?

45

With Knowledge comes Control.
Perhaps it's just a fallacy,
But if we had Cassandra's Knowledge
We might be able to control the galaxy.

46

But enough about the Future.
And our Universal Fate.
Without the Knowledge of Cassandra
We can only watch and wait.

47

It is difficult to create a myth
About what the Universe has or lacks;
But a myth about the Human Past
Can be brought in line with the facts.

48

Apollo was a god among the gods.
His pedigree was impeccable.
He had power over the Human World
But his use of that power was execrable.

49

He thought that he could control The Myth
Of the Story of the Trojan War –
The myth about he and Cassandra
He thought would live forever more.

50

But the joke is on Apollo.
He tried to keep Cassandra down.
Now his name will live in Infamy
And her name will live in Renown.

51

We are all jagged stones –
Life makes smooth stones of us.
In Cassandra's case,
Life ground her into dust.

52

And there you have it – A Woman –
Diminished – held back – stifled.
All that she had accomplished was –
By A Man – denigrated and trifled.

53

Good writing conquers bad writing.
Good myth erases bad myth.
We can update The Cassandra Story –
Tell the story that Homer missed.

54

It is Humans who write the myths –
A fact that Homer knew.
He sang, as he strummed beside the ashes,
The story he thought was true.

55

But now we have altered that ancient story –
Taken Homer's Presentation –
And added some pertinent details
To make it A Myth for our Generation.

56

Good myth can conquer bad myth.
Time to give Cassandra her due:
The Most Knowledgeable Person – Man or Woman –
That the World Ever Knew.

Three Books

The Story

The writer, John Passfield, contemplates writing a novel about Cassandra. Suddenly, he finds himself in the presence of her tormentor, Apollo, the god who – seemingly as a whim – has brought a catastrophic curse down on the head of an innocent human. John sees Cassandra as a mythical creature whose helpless situation contains the dynamics of all that is wrong on the planet Earth. What a chance to confront a representative of the gods and ask him to explain such actions and to demand an immediate end to all the agony in the world.

The Making of Fair Is Fair

This journal records the author's reflections on the process of the crafting of the novel as it evolved through the stages of planning, writing, editing and polishing. It constitutes an effort to be as conscious as possible of the process whereby the single idea that suggested the topic of the novel was expanded into a complex work of art. Topics range from the nuts and bolts of novel-building to the nature of the novel as an art-form.

Planning Fair Is Fair

During the writing of the novel, the author kept a hand-written notebook which records the day-by-day development of the novel as it found its shape and style. The notebook – now in print form – reveals how a vast cluster of thoughts was sifted, selected, structured and polished into novel-form.

The Project

Together, this novel, journal and notebook comprise the thirty-first installment in an on-going novel-writing project in which the author is exploring the concept of form and meaning in the novel, and of the novel as a form of expression in the 21st century. All of the published journals and notebooks are available for free download.

About the Author

John Passfield was born in St. Thomas, Ontario, Canada, and continues to reside in Southern Ontario, near Cayuga, with his family. He is interested in exploring the development of the novel as an art-form, and has written many novels, planning notebooks and journals in his search for a form for the poetic novel of our time. His novel *John Passfield: Saturday Morning* was shortlisted for the ReLit Award in 2022.

Novels by John Passfield

Grave Song
The Agony of Robert Chisholm

Jumbo
P. T. Barnum's Greatest Creation

Pinafore Park
The Swan Boat Incident

Water Lane
The Pilgrimage of Christopher Marlowe

Rain of Fire
The Ordeal of Conductor Spettigue

Victoria Day
The Fabric of the Community

The Wright Brothers
Flight is Possible

Leni Riefenstahl
The Valley of the Shadow

Babe Ruth
Out of the Park

Raskolnikov
Murder with an Axe

Sergei Eisenstein
Death Day

Albert Einstein
Wonder

Geoffrey Chaucer
Canterbury Bound

Ospringe
A Visit with Grandad

Pompeii
Vesuvius Dominus

Beethoven
The Ninth Immersion

Job
The Cornerstone of the Universe

Bethune
The Only Person Alive in the World

Terry Fox
Somewhere the Hurting Must Stop

Lord and Lady Macbeth
Full of Scorpions Is My Mind

Cyril Passfield
Out West

Glenn Gould
Light and Dark

Emily Brontë
More Myself Than I

L. M. Montgomery
I Gave You Life

Pauline Johnson
Know Who I Am

John Passfield
Saturday Morning

Eleonora Duse
Let Me Have My Wings

James McIntyre
The Mammoth Cheese

Shakespeare and Cleopatra
My Life Is Not My Own

John and Santa
The Cowboy Shirt

John and Cassandra
Fair is Fair

John and Dickens
A Christmas Mystery

John and Lewis Carroll
Wonder Fall

John and Mother Goose
The Carnival of Tales

John and the Universan
Nothing is Known

Chatterton
A Self of My Own

See www.johnpassfield.ca for publishing information.

In Search of Form and Meaning:
Journals by John Passfield

Each journal is a day-by-day record of the complex process that a writer undergoes while crafting a work of art. It records the largest decisions, of structure and theme, and the smallest decisions, such as the choice of one word over another, and the constant interaction between the two. Each journal is a record of a writer's reflection on the craft of novel-writing.

The Making of Grave Song

The Making of Jumbo

The Making of Pinafore Park

The Making of Water Lane

The Making of Rain of Fire

The Making of Victoria Day

The Making of Flight is Possible

The Making of The Valley of the Shadow

The Making of Out of the Park

The Making of Murder with an Axe

The Making of Death Day

The Making of Wonder

The Making of Canterbury Bound

The Making of Ospringe

The Making of Vesuvius Dominus

The Making of The Ninth Immersion

The Making of The Cornerstone of the Universe

The Making of The Only Person Alive in the World

The Making of Somewhere the Hurting Must Stop

The Making of Full of Scorpions Is My Mind

The Making of Out West

The Making of Glenn Gould: Light and Dark

The Making of Emily Brontë: More Myself Than I

The Making of Pauline Johnson: Know Who I Am

The Making of John Passfield: Saturday Morning

The Making of Eleonora Duse: Let Me Have My Wings

The Making of James McIntyre: The Mammoth Cheese

The Making of Shakespeare and Cleopatra: My Life Is Not My Own

The Making of John and Santa: The Cowboy Shirt

The Making of John and Cassandra: Fair is Fair

The Making of John and Dickens: A Christmas Mystery

The Making of John and Lewis Carroll: Wonder Fall

The Making of John and Mother Goose: The Carnival of Tales

The Making of John and the Universan: Nothing is Known

The Making of Chatterton: A Self of My Own

See www.johnpassfield.ca for publishing information.

The Novel as an Art-Form:
Planning Notebooks by John Passfield

Each planning notebook is a printed version of the hand-written notebook which records the planning, writing, editing and polishing of each novel. Each notebook is an attempt to record, understand, and organize the vast cluster of thoughts which occur as one grapples with the various levels of organization which a clear yet complex work of art demands.

Planning Grave Song

Planning Jumbo

Planning Pinafore Park

Planning Water Lane

Planning Rain of Fire

Planning Victoria Day

Planning Flight is Possible

Planning The Valley of the Shadow

Planning Out of the Park

Planning Murder with an Axe

Planning Death Day

Planning Wonder

Planning Canterbury Bound

Planning Ospringe

Planning Vesuvius Dominus

Planning The Ninth Immersion

Planning The Cornerstone of the Universe

Planning The Only Person Alive in the World

Planning Somewhere the Hurting Must Stop

Planning Full of Scorpions Is My Mind

Planning Out West

Planning Glenn Gould: Light and Dark

Planning Emily Brontë: More Myself Than I

Planning L. M. Montgomery: I Gave You Life

Planning Pauline Johnson: Know Who I Am

Planning John Passfield: Saturday Morning

Planning Eleonora Duse: Let Me Have My Wings

Planning James McIntyre: The Mammoth Cheese

Planning Shakespeare and Cleopatra: My Life Is Not My Own

Planning John and Santa: The Cowboy Shirt

Planning John and Cassandra: Fair is Fair

Planning John and Dickens: A Christmas Mystery

Planning John and Lewis Carroll: Wonder Fall

Planning John and Mother Goose: The Carnival of Tales

Planning John and the Universan: Nothing is Known

Planning Chatterton: A Self of My Own

See www.johnpassfield.ca for publishing information.

Other Books
by John Passfield

Oak Street
The Passfield Family

The Poetic Novel I
Influences and Elements

Intensities I
Verses on Various Topics

Intensities II
Verses on Various Topics

Deepening Imagery I
Verses from the Novels

Deepening Imagery II
Verses from the Novels

Deepening Imagery III
Verses from the Novels

Deepening Imagery IV
Verses from the Novels

Video-notes I
(1–100)

Video-notes II
(101–200)

See www.johnpassfield.ca for free access.